# ABOUT THE AUTHOR

Following his law degree where he developed an interest in criminal law, Matt Brolly completed his Masters in Creative Writing at Glasgow University.

He is the bestselling author of the DCI Lambert crime novels, Dead Eyed, Dead Lucky, Dead Embers, and Dead Time as well as the acclaimed near future crime novel, Zero, and the US thriller, The Controller.

In 2020 the first of a new crime series set in the West Country of the UK will be released by Thomas and Mercer (Amazon Publishing)

Matt also writes children's books as M.J. Brolly. His first children's book, The Sleeping Bug, was released by Oblong Books in December 2018.

Matt lives in London with his wife and their two young children. You can find out more about Matt at his website www.mattbrolly.co.uk or by following him on twitter: @MattBrollyUK

# ALSO BY MATT BROLLY

## DCI LAMBERT NOVELS:

DEAD EYED - DCI LAMBERT BOOK 1

DEAD LUCKY - DCI LAMBERT BOOK 2

DEAD EMBERS - DCI LAMBERT BOOK 3

DEAD TIME - DCI LAMBERT BOOK 4

## OTHER NOVELS

ZERO

THE CONTROLLER

THE CROSSING

First published in the United Kingdom in 2019 by Oblong Books
Copyright © 2019 by Matt Brolly
The moral right of Matt Brolly to be identified as the author of this work has
been asserted in accordance with the Copyright, Designs and Patents Act,
1988.
A CIP catalogue record for this book is available from the British Library.
978-0-9957747-6-6  ·

*For Michael Brolly*

# PROLOGUE

The pub was stationed less than a hundred yards from Belmarsh prison in southeast London. Detective Chief Superintendent Glenn Tillman had called in a favour and shut down the place for the day. A hush descended over the room as, head bowed, Alice Fowler opened the door, followed by her mother.

The situation was a first for DCI Michael Lambert. While Alice had spent the last hour in the prison for the parole hearing of Joseph Wyatt, Lambert had been in the bar with Alice's father and the families of the victims.

Twenty-five years ago, Joseph Wyatt had been convicted for the murder of two young women and the attempted murder of Alice Fowler. Like his victims, Wyatt had been a member of the university rowing team.

Lambert was at a table with Tillman and the two former officers who'd arrested Wyatt.

'How did it go, dear?' asked Alice's father, Tom.

Alice crashed down onto a chair as if her legs had been kicked away from her. 'I hardly recognised him, he's changed so much.' she said, downing the offered vodka in one quick gulp.

Tillman walked from behind the bar and placed a second drink in front of Alice. 'What happened?' he asked Alice's mother.

'He was still being questioned when we left. Alice and I read out our statements.' The woman hung onto the solid arm of her husband, who stared ahead with stoic intensity. His air of hostility hadn't faded since earlier in the morning when they'd first gathered. He'd appeared to be on a hair trigger, and Lambert had been waiting for the man to explode ever since.

'You should have seen him,' said Mrs Fowler, shaking her head. 'I'm scared, Tom,' she said to her husband, as if they were alone. 'He was acting like he was sorry, that he regretted everything and I think they believed him.'

'Didn't they listen to what you said?' asked Tom Fowler.

'I told them the impact he had on our lives, Dad,' said Alice. 'On everyone's lives,' she added, glancing at the families of the other victims, who had not been so fortunate. 'It's up to them now.'

Tom Fowler went behind the bar and poured some more vodka. 'You can't let this happen,' he said to Tillman.

'Let's wait and see what they come back with, Mr Fowler,' said Tillman.

'When will we know?' said Tom Fowler.

'They have fourteen days but I'll find out earlier. I promise you all, I will notify you as soon as I know,' said Tillman.

Lambert stood as the families filtered out. The signs of loss were unmistakable and Lambert thought about his daughter, Chloe, and how inconceivable it would be to live without her. The families exchanged words with Tillman and the other officers until only the Fowlers were left.

Tom Fowler offered his hand to Tillman, the hardness still in his eyes. They looked like a close-knit family but Wyatt's attack had impacted them as much as the others. Alice had dropped out of university, and had suffered from depression ever since. Lambert understood Mr Fowler's anger. Wyatt's attacks had been savage. Alice's witness statement recalled in terrifying detail how he'd attacked her by the river, the grip of his hands against her throat as he'd held her under the water, the attack made worse by the fact she knew and trusted her assailant. And she was the lucky one, the one still alive to tell the tale. 'I wanted him to rot in there,' said Fowler.

'We all did,' said Tillman, breaking free of the handshake.

Tillman was Lambert's direct supervisor within a specialised division of the Serious Organised Crime Agency (SOCA) known as the Group. He'd suggested Lambert attend as a neutral observer but this cold case had no relevance to Lambert and he wanted to be away from the graveyard feel, and return to work on the numerous cases that needed his urgent attention.

Once the families were gone, Tillman retrieved a bottle of whisky from behind the bar and placed it on the table. The only people left were Tillman's two former colleagues from the investigation, Mark Devlin and Terry Kirby - and Dan Hogg, a journalist who was friends with the trio, and who'd reported on the Wyatt case.

Lambert wanted to object but Kirby had already started pouring the drinks. Reluctantly, Lambert joined the four men in a silent toast.

'He hasn't changed,' Tillman said eventually, undoing his

top button. Tillman had the upper body of a body builder, albeit one who was slightly out of shape. Yet he still insisted on wearing shirts one size too small for him.

'Remember when we brought him in?' said Kirby, his mouth half full of whisky. 'Absolutely no remorse for what he'd done.'

'He was proud. Thought he was something special. Those poor girls,' said Devlin.

Tillman's eyes lowered but he didn't comment.

'You reported on it?' Lambert asked the journalist, Hogg, who'd been silent ever since Alice Fowler had returned.

'First major case.'

Lambert looked over at Tillman who was unusually silent. 'You all knew each other before though?'

'We were at university together.'

Lambert smiled at the idea of Tillman being at university. He couldn't picture his superior at lectures, or even at a student bar. He viewed Tillman as someone who'd been fully formed as a policeman and struggled to imagine him listening to anyone else's opinion. 'So you three joined the Met, and you became a journalist?'

'He couldn't hack real life, even back then, could you Hoggy?' said Kirby.

Hogg sighed and drank some whisky. 'I wanted to write about corruption not be at the heart of it,' he said, with a wry smile.

'Didn't have the balls,' said Kirby.

'Remind me what you do again, Terry?' said Hogg.

'Why did Wyatt do it?' asked Lambert, desperate to change the tone of the souring conversation.

'His mother drowned when he was a child,' said Hogg.

'Bullshit,' said Devlin. 'He was a sick little bastard who couldn't get a girlfriend. Probably couldn't get it up either.'

'He played the mental health card but thankfully they didn't fall for it. Now he's a reformed character by all accounts. Found God and whatnot. You should do a piece on him, Hogg,' said Kirby, not hiding his disdain.

The animosity was palpable. Lambert had noticed the gentle ribbing between the four men earlier, but much of it was now centred on the journalist, the teasing suddenly closer to bullying.

'Perhaps we should think about heading off, Sir,' said Lambert.

Tillman scowled and poured everyone another drink, no one prepared to argue with him.

Reluctantly, Lambert accepted the whisky. He was still confused by his role as neutral observer. Until yesterday, he'd never heard of the case, and Tillman hadn't supplied him with any details beyond the basics.

'What happened on the night you found Wyatt?' he asked. Tillman wasn't a talker. Lambert knew very little about the man personally. He was a diligent professional, had more contacts than anyone Lambert had ever worked with, but this was as much as he'd ever seen of Tillman's personal side. With the drink flowing, he sensed an opportunity.

'It was an oversight,' said Kirby, receiving a warning glance from Tillman.

'There was no oversight. We'd interviewed Wyatt like we'd interviewed all their friends. There was no way of knowing,' said Tillman.

Lambert rarely heard his boss sounding defensive. 'What tipped you off?'

Tillman and the two retired officers exchanged looks,

whilst Hogg sipped at his whisky. Lambert could tell by Till-man's pained expression he didn't want to talk further but risked the appearance of being weak if he backed down now in front of his friends. 'Simon Travis.'

'Travis?'

'He was a forensic psychologist who'd been assigned to the department. Suggested we start looking for potential suspects who had an affinity with water, who'd possibly suffered some trauma. It was a fluke really. All the girls were members of this bloody rowing club so we didn't know where to start. Then we spotted that Wyatt's mother had drowned when he was a child. Travis agreed this may have acted as a catalyst, and that our original questioning of him could have been more detailed.'

'Even then we didn't believe it,' said Devlin.

Tillman frowned at his former colleague as if he'd spoken out of turn. 'The club was meeting that night. I went down to see them only to be told that Wyatt and Alice had headed off together.'

'Funny how things work out,' said Hogg.

'What the fuck does that mean?' said Tillman to the journalist, a gnarled vein prominent on his forehead.

'It doesn't mean anything. I'm just suggesting that if you'd been any later you wouldn't have caught them and Alice wouldn't be alive.'

Tillman didn't look placated. Lambert wondered what had so riled his superior, and where the animosity towards the journalist came from. 'I found them by an old boathouse. He had her by the throat in the water. He was weak at that point so it was easy enough to drag him off her. Claimed it was an accident, can you believe that? He was holding her under the water and still claimed it was an accident,' said

Tillman, filling his glass and taking another mouthful of whisky as if it was medicine.

'We should have put him out of his misery,' said Kirby.

Tillman glanced at Lambert as if embarrassed by Kirby's outburst. 'He got what he deserved.'

The call came in an hour later. Lambert watched the tension build in Tillman's face, growing steady as he listened to the bad news. He hung up without speaking, launching the phone into the row of optics behind the bar. Somehow the phone bounced off the glass bottles and landed without smashing on the floor. Tillman hurdled over the bar after it, and ripped a bottle of single malt from the optic holder swigging from it as if it was water.

'It won't be official for two weeks,' he said. 'But they're going to release Wyatt on parole.'

# 1

ONE YEAR LATER

CHIEF SUPERINTENDENT TILLMAN'S former boss, a wily old soak by the name of Jenkins, had often liked to hypothesise on defining moments. For Jenkins, his defining moment had been leaving his wife and children. 'It's been the making of me,' he'd told Tillman, one smoke-filled night in the old bar close to Scotland Yard where Tillman had spent the majority of his twenties.

Jenkins had delusions of grandeur, believing his role in the Met to have had much greater significance than it did. He'd retired ten years later, overweight and alone. Yet, his words haunted Tillman as he walked the unlit street back to his flat. Had his defining moment occurred twenty-four years ago by the bank of the Thames? He'd had choices then and, although he cared little for regrets, he thought now that maybe he'd made the wrong decision.

Joseph Wyatt had disappeared six months after his release and now Devlin and Kirby were dead. Tillman was in charge of the hunt for Wyatt but he feared that was about to change. He had a meeting with the Chief Constable tomorrow morning and suspected the case was going to be taken from him. It was a wonder he'd held onto it for so long. He was the obvious next victim and had been forced to turn down the offer of protection on a number of occasions since Kirby's body was discovered three weeks ago.

He hated feeling this way. Usually he would walk through the shortcut near his flat without a second thought. He didn't think Wyatt would attack him - he had no real reason - yet he waited for the former prisoner around every corner.

More annoyed than scared, Tillman cursed the way his hand flinched, and his heart started beating harder, when a fox surprised him by scurrying out from the shadows.

Crossing the road, relieved to be under the streetlights, Tillman took his front door key from his pocket. His gaze distracted by a light shining against the pane of the front window, he thought back to that night. Maybe Devlin and Kirby had been right after all. If he'd only listened back then they wouldn't be dead, and he wouldn't be acting like a coward.

You had to hand it to Wyatt. He'd fooled them all and now this coup de grace. He'd killed both Devlin and Kirby by drowning, after keeping them captive for exactly seven days. It was a perfect irony though perhaps not in the way everyone else thought. Devlin and Kirby had taken a secret with them to their watery grave, one only Wyatt, Tillman, and one other now knew.

The presumption was that Wyatt came after the two

former officers because they'd been the ones who'd arrested him.

However, Tillman knew different, and that was why he was surprised to see the man emerge from the shadows and plunge the syringe in his neck before he had a chance to respond.

Lambert received the summons at eight am, a coded message on his phone instructing him to get to the office immediately. Lambert swore to himself as he took a swig of lukewarm coffee.

'What did you say, Daddy?' asked Chloe, his five year old daughter.

'You have the ears of a bat,' said Lambert.

'A bat?' said Chloe, biting down on a piece of toast as she studied her father.

'It's a saying,' said Lambert, scrolling through the address book on his phone. Chloe wasn't due at school for another hour and his wife, Sophie, had already left for work. 'Listen, darling, I'm going to have to drop you off early at school.'

'What?' said Chloe, her incredulity making Lambert smile.

'They have that breakfast club thing, don't they? I'm really sorry but they need me at work.'

Chloe glared at him. Even aged five, he couldn't always tell when she was truly angry or just playing games with him.

'You owe me,' she said, leaving the table and pulling her coat on.

'Owe you? Where did you hear that?'

'You said it to Mummy the other night,' said Chloe, pleased with herself.

Lambert sighed. 'Like a bat,' he said, shaking his head.

It was ninety minutes before he reached the tube station at Angel in Islington. It was an early spring morning, the sun beginning to burn through the clouds. Lambert called Tillman on the way in but his phone had gone straight to answerphone.

He'd spent the last few months working on finding Wyatt with his boss. Lambert had some grave reservations about their work. His main concern centred on the fact that Wyatt's latest victims were Tillman's former colleagues, Devlin and Kirby, who he'd met the previous year during the parole hearing for Joseph Wyatt. Tillman was too close to the investigation and Lambert was surprised he'd been given the case in the first place.

Well, as surprised as he could ever be when it came to Tillman. In the three years Lambert had been part of Tillman's team, it had become apparent Tillman had carte blanche to do whatever he wanted. The Group's secret headquarters were fitted out with top of the range equipment, and Tillman, at least on the surface, didn't appear to report to anyone.

The incident room was set up in a secret location in a serviced office building five minutes' walk from the tube station. Lambert greeted the security guard by the front desk and took the lift to the fifth floor where he was presented with a door protected by an electronic identification system.

Lambert punched in his eight-digit code and opened the door, immediately wishing he'd stayed at home.

'Sir?' said Lambert.

He'd only met the Chief Constable, Adam Hickman, twice before and had never spoken to the man. It was bizarre seeing him in the office, stranger still to see him completely alone. 'DCI Michael Lambert?' said Hickman.

'Sir.'

'So this is Tillman's little hideout,' said Hickman, getting to his feet and pacing the room. He studied the various images on the murder walls: photographs of Kirby and Devlin, next to the original victims Michelle Lewis and Lisa Bradford from twenty-five years ago, and to one side the only person so far to have escaped Wyatt, Alice Fowler.

'Sir.'

'How the hell they ever let that animal out, I'll never know.'

'Is there something I should be made aware of, sir?' asked Lambert.

'Now that you ask, there is. I was supposed to meet Chief Superintendent Glenn Tillman this morning for breakfast but he didn't turn up. His phone goes straight to answerphone and he is not at his flat. I sent two of my officers around and the damage to the shrubbery outside his place suggests he may have been involved in some form of struggle.'

'Shit,' said Lambert.

'Shit indeed. So I take it from that you haven't heard from him?'

'No, sir.'

'Then I'm afraid we have to presume that Chief Superintendent Tillman is missing. We further have to work on the basis that we will discover his body in seven days if we don't find him.'

Lambert had warned Tillman but he wouldn't listen. It made perfect sense for Wyatt to come after him next. He'd killed two of the three men who'd put him behind bars, so why not the third? Tillman had told him they didn't have the resources, but Lambert didn't think that wasn't the reason Tillman hadn't wanted security. The man was under the illusion that he was invincible.

The reference to finding the body in seven days related to the bodies of Kirby and Devlin each turning up seven days after they'd gone missing. 'What a mess.'

'Yes, what a mess.'

Hickman was about to elaborate when another member of the Group, DI Adrienne Corrigan, joined them. Adrienne was the oldest member of the Group. Close to retirement age, she was the hardest working officer Lambert had ever encountered. She lived at headquarters - always there in the morning when he arrived, still there when he left. 'Michael,' she said.

'At present, only you, DI Corrigan, and I know about this. I want it to stay that way. I don't want the press getting hold of this, do you understand, DCI Lambert?'

The press would get to hear about it if Tillman's body was washed up on the Thames but Lambert wasn't about to tell the Chief that. 'Sir.'

'I've just been to Glenn's flat. Definite sign of a struggle. 'I've canvassed the whole area but no witnesses,' said Adrienne.

'With all due respect, sir, do you think we are the best section to handle this case,' said Lambert. He would do everything in his power to find Tillman, but having his superior's existing team on the investigation felt like a conflict of interest.

Hickman shook his head, the fluorescent light catching the skin of the bald patch on his thinning grey hair. 'You're the right man, Lambert. With your background and DI Corrigan's...diligence, you have all the resources you need. Get your colleagues in but keep this in house.'

'You want us to manage this alone?'

'If you need extra resources contact me. I will provide them, but no one is to know about this. I expect a report at the end of play each day,' said Hickman, walking towards the door. 'And Lambert?'

'Sir.'

'I expect you to find him,' said Hickman, his words laden with threat.

Lambert collapsed onto the nearest seat. Although part of him expected it, he couldn't believe Tillman had been taken. The man's self-belief was so forceful that Lambert had bought into his invincibility. He half expected Tillman to burst through the door, his shirt pulled tight against his considerable bulk, and demand Lambert get back to work.

'When did you find out about this?' he asked Adrienne.

'Not long before you. I was at the meeting with Hickman waiting for Glenn to arrive.'

'He's definitely missing?'

Adrienne didn't answer. Lambert acknowledged he'd asked a stupid question. He glanced at the various murder boards, at the images already ingrained into his memory. The Chief's threat had been all too clear. Lambert would take the blame if Tillman wasn't found. It was career-defining. It was unfair but Lambert was used to such injustices. He was presented with them on a daily basis, pieces of bureaucracy that hindered his job and made him wonder about his career choice.

Where to turn to now? Wyatt had gone missing six months ago. Tillman had led the investigation into his disappearance immediately after Wyatt missed his first probation meeting. He would have been returned to prison for breaking his terms of release and initially it had been viewed as a good thing. But the man simply vanished. Wyatt had left all his stuff at his room at the halfway house, even £35 in cash. He'd left in a hurry, and the initial working theory had been that he'd taken his own life. But then, three months later, the body of Mark Devlin had been found by the river in Rotherhithe.

If the deaths of Tillman's former colleagues had taken an emotional toll on Lambert's superior, he'd hidden it well. It was all about work for him, and his passion for that was always relentless. The death of Terry Kirby a month later only strengthened his conviction to find Wyatt. On the rare moments he'd managed to speak to Tillman on a personal level, he'd always avoid talking about his time together with Devlin and Kirby. Unless it was relevant to finding Wyatt, and in Tillman's view it wasn't, he hadn't wanted to discuss it.

Adrienne wasn't the sort of officer Lambert had felt comfortable discussing Tillman's emotional state with during the investigation. She wasn't exactly cold but she was more pragmatic than he was. She would see Tillman's emotional state as an irrelevance to the pressing matter in hand. 'Where do you want to start?' he asked.

'I've made a list of tasks. Usual procedure. I am going to speak to the families of Kirby and Devlin. It's a long shot but they might know something. Anything you can add?'

Lambert glanced at the operations manual Adrienne had

already put together for him, the list of people they needed to speak to, the locations to be visited. He thought back to that time at the bar, awaiting news on Wyatt's parole meeting. And afterwards with the doors locked, Tillman sucking down whisky like water with Devlin and Kirby. Aside from Lambert, the only man who'd been present that night who wasn't either dead or missing was Daniel Hogg. 'I need to speak to the journalist,' he said, Adrienne already heading towards the door. She nodded and left as Lambert cranked opened his laptop and located an office address for the man.

## 3

Tillman had never experienced pain like it. He'd never given it much thought but within SOCA he had the reputation of being a hard man. People thought of him as an 'old school' copper. He didn't like the association. To his mind it suggested he was behind the times, was prepared to step over the line to get things done. He would rather be known as hard but fair, but as the man placed the cloth over his face for a second time all thoughts about being tough vanished. He was a trembling wreck and wanted it over. Better the man take his life than make him endure another second of this.

Unfortunately, his captor wasn't attuned to Tillman's feelings. Without a word, he began pouring water over the cloth. Tillman tried not to panic but it was impossible. Later he would marvel it how effective such a simple technique could be. For now, he began thrashing in his restraints as he felt the weight of the world push down onto his chest, his lungs bursting.

'There, there,' said the man, lifting the rag from his face.

Tillman gasped for air like a fish plucked from the sea. It

felt like he'd endured the waterboarding for minutes when it had probably been only seconds. That was why the torture was so effective. They said it mimicked the sensation of drowning. If that was the case, then the theory that drowning was a pleasant way to die was far off the mark.

'Why are you doing this?' he asked his assailant, disgusted with the whine he heard in his voice. The man had to be Wyatt. He had yet to reveal his face, but who else could it be?

Devlin and Kirby had been found seven days after they'd gone missing. Wyatt hadn't killed them immediately, their autopsies suggesting they died within twenty-four hours of their bodies being discovered. And although that gave Tillman another six days, if the last few minutes were anything to go by, the next week was likely to be the worst of his life.

The masked figure looked down on him.

'Why don't you end it?' demanded Tillman, his body still trembling from the waterboarding.

'You haven't suffered enough yet,' said Wyatt. 'You should have ended it when you had the chance.'

# 4

Lambert took the Docklands Light Railway to Canary Wharf. Although the DLR had been in operation for over two decades, the journey into East London always felt like something out of a JG Ballard novel. The silent hum of the driverless carriages ushered him across the river Thames, past giant glass buildings. There was a clinical coldness to the place, a sense of loneliness to the nondescript office blocks and the worker ants occupying them.

The broadsheet newspaper's headquarters was in One Canada Square with its distinctive pyramid roof. The original skyscraper of the Isle of Dogs was still the tallest building in the skyline despite the numerous competing buildings that had sprouted up over the years. Lambert hadn't called ahead so was stopped by a jobsworth security guard in the foyer of the building, a large open spaced area with marbled floors. 'I can't let you up without a pass,' said the guard, when Lambert flashed him his warrant card.

'I'm here to see Daniel Hogg,' said Lambert.

'Do you know which floor he works on?'

'No,' said Lambert, matching the guard's gaze until he looked away.

Eventually the guard relented and located Hogg, asking Lambert politely to take a seat.

Ten minutes later, the journalist appeared. Ashen-faced, his forehead was damp with perspiration as if he'd sprinted down the steps from his office. 'DCI Lambert, this is a surprise. Everything ok?' he asked, holding out his hand.

His handshake was weak, his palm coated in sweat. 'Is there somewhere we can speak in private?' asked Lambert.

'Of course.'

Another painful five minutes passed as Lambert was given security clearance and a tag to wear around his neck. Hogg led him to the elevators that shared the same gentle hum of the DLR as they rose into the heights of the tower. Lambert caught the faint whiff of alcohol on the man. 'You enjoy working here?' asked Lambert.

'The novelty wears off pretty soon, especially in rush hour,' said Hogg, giving way to Lambert as the lift doors eased open.

Hogg led him through the journalists' equivalent of a bullpen, an open planned office space where Hogg's colleagues stared at digital screens whilst battering their keyboards. It was a far cry from the Fleet Street offices Lambert recalled from his early years on the force. The smoke filled rooms where the journos battled with the thick keys on their typewriters. 'Is this free, Maggie?' Hogg asked a young woman, in a tailored trouser suit.

'It's needed in thirty minutes,' said the woman, disappearing into the main office.

'Can I get you anything?' asked Hogg, as they sat.

Behind Hogg, the small window gave stunning views of the meandering river and the millennium dome.

'I'm fine,' said Lambert.

'Is this about the Wyatt case?' said Hogg.

'This is strictly off the record, Mr Hogg.'

'I understand and call me Dan. You've seen me pissed out of my mind. I consider you a friend.'

Lambert stared at Hogg, appraising him. He was the same age as Tillman but had aged badly. His skin was ragged and pitted, a swirling grey mess of hair covered his scalp in uneven patches, and his ruby red nose marked him out as a drinker. He'd been drunk that time at the bar, but they all had, the bottle of whisky not lasting long as Tillman continually filled their glasses like an over-enthusiastic waiter. Lambert remembered what the Chief Constable had told him. Tillman's disappearance was supposed to be a secret, but here he was in the heart of a press building talking to a journalist about it. 'It's more than off the record. What I'm about to tell you can go no further than this room.'

Although Hogg had run the story on the original Wyatt killings, he'd declined the opportunity to report on the deaths of Devlin and Kirby. Unlike Tillman, he felt his relationship to the two men made it a conflict of interests. 'I understand. You have my word.'

Lambert studied the man as he told him about Tillman's disappearance. Aside from a slight twitch in his right eye, Hogg gave little away.

'You sure he's actually missing? It wouldn't be the first time Glenn went AWOL.'

'We're sure.'

Hogg pinched his nose, his pallid features somehow losing more colour as the full extent of the situation hit him. 'I find this all so surreal. A year ago that maniac was still in prison and now...now I am going to lose another friend.'

Despite his words, Lambert wasn't convinced Hogg was being genuine. 'There could still be time, Dan. I need to know everything you know about Wyatt, about what happened that first time around.'

Hogg sighed, the sound low and haunted as if Tillman's fate was completely in his hands. 'What do you know about Wyatt's arrest on the night Alice Fowler was rescued?'

Lambert had read the three officer reports from that night in detail as well as the testimony of Alice Fowler. 'Tillman went to the rowing club to question Wyatt, only to discover that Wyatt had headed off with Alice Fowler. Tillman had tracked the pair to the old boathouse in Fulham, arriving in time to rescue Alice Fowler from her attacker.'

'Anything ever strike you as strange about that whole scenario?'

'You mean how easy it was to locate Wyatt?'

'Exactly. Even if he'd got away with killing Alice, everyone knew he was the last person to be with her. He would have become a suspect either way.'

'You think he wanted to get caught?' asked Lambert.

'I think he wanted to stop doing what he was doing. Remember, Michelle Lewis's death was technically manslaughter.'

That much was true. Michelle Lewis was Wyatt's first victim though he was never convicted of her murder. He'd claimed he hadn't meant to kill her. They'd been playing by the river and things had got out of hand. In his own words, he'd held her under the water to see what she'd look like. When he'd let her go, it had been too late. Wyatt admitted to the murder of Lisa Bradford, the second victim, and the attempted murder of Alice Fowler so the conviction of manslaughter for Michelle Lewis was easier for the prosecution to accept. 'So why the hell has he started doing it all again?'

Hogg groaned as he stood up. He placed his palms against the window of the office, bent over as if the wind had been knocked out of him. 'There's something Glenn never told you about that night. It's not in the reports and he only told me one night when he was drunk. I'm not sure he even remembers telling me.'

It was Lambert's turn to sigh. 'What happened?'

Hogg was too far in now not to tell him. 'After dragging Wyatt off Alice, Glenn was left to tend to her on the shore while they waited for an ambulance and back up.'

'And?' said Lambert, sensing he didn't want to hear what the journalist was about to tell him.

'Remember, Devlin and Kirby were present by this time. They decided to mete out some justice of their own on Wyatt. They took turns dunking him in the river.'

Lambert shook his head. He didn't condone the behaviour, was surprised Tillman had let them get away with it. It was pointless to ask why Wyatt hadn't mentioned it during the trial. With two dead women it was unlikely his story would be believed. 'There's more?'

'It went too far. Alice was out cold. Devlin and Kirby wanted to end it.'

'End it?'

Hogg struggled to maintain eye contact with him. 'They wanted to kill Wyatt, to blame it on the struggle when they'd pulled him off Alice. It was dark and secluded. There were no witnesses.'

   'Tillman stopped them?'

   'He did, but he told me he wasn't sure he'd made the right decision.'

## 5

Lambert wasn't sure he believed what Hogg was trying to tell him. Why hadn't Tillman mentioned any of this before? Lambert could understand a desire to protect his former colleagues, but if what Hogg said was true - that Devlin and Kirby really had tried to kill Wyatt - then it gave the former convict an extra motive to exact revenge on the men.

'In the end, I think that was why Devlin and Kirby left the force,' said Hogg.

Lambert had forgotten the journalist was still in his room. 'You think Tillman pressured them to leave?'

'I know he felt guilty for what they'd done. That he didn't report it.'

'You ever get these events verified from anyone else?'

'No.'

Now the only person aside from Tillman who could verify the story was Alice Fowler and according to Hogg, and the original police report, she'd been unconscious after Tillman had rescued her. 'What aren't you telling me, Dan?'

'I'm telling you everything I know. More than I should.'

'More than you should? Two men are dead and your friend is missing. You should have volunteered this information much sooner.'

'So should Tillman.'

'That doesn't make this right. If you're withholding something from me now there will be consequences, do you understand?'

Hogg squirmed. At the bar, on the day of Wyatt's parole hearing, Lambert had sensed the tension between Hogg and the other three men. He was beginning to see something in the journalist he didn't like which would explain the animosity from the other three men. 'Did you hold the knowledge over them, Dan?'

Hogg repeated his squinting gesture. 'What do you mean?'

'Devlin and Kirby's attack on Wyatt. When I met you all, Kirby and Devlin didn't appear to have any issue with Tillman. They were getting along fine, each with a common enemy. You.'

Hogg shook his head as if Lambert had missed something obvious. 'It wasn't that type of relationship. We were thrown together at university. I never really considered myself their friend. Of the three of them, I got along with Glenn the best.'

'Why did you hang round with them then?'

'Force of habit. You fall into these types of unhealthy relationships. In retrospect, Kirby and Devlin were bullies. I hadn't realised it at the time. I saw it when they joined the police and I reported their cases.'

'You not keen on the police, Dan?'

'I have nothing against the police but people like Kirby and Devlin had no place in such an organisation.'

'And Tillman?'

'I don't think Glenn really understood what they were like until the night of Wyatt's arrest.'

LAMBERT CAUGHT the DLR back towards the city. In its place was a growing melancholy. He wished Tillman had told him what had happened that night by the river. Did he think Lambert would judge him? Lambert had seen many officers lose their rag at a crime scene, especially when something horrific had occurred to a victim. It was human nature. But there was a line, and if Kirby and Devlin had really threatened to kill Wyatt then it clouded things.

He'd arranged to meet Aaron Davenport, Wyatt's parole officer, at a small coffee shop in Islington. Tillman had met the man after Wyatt absconded, and twice more after Devlin and Kirby's murders but Lambert hadn't been present either time. Lambert recognised Davenport's face from a photograph in Wyatt's file. He was a gaunt, nervous-looking man sitting at the front of the shop, his finger tracing the circumference of the top of his coffee cup. 'Aaron Davenport?' asked Lambert.

Davenport looked up from his cup. 'Yes, yes,' he stammered. 'DCI Lambert?'

Lambert nodded. 'Another one of those?' he asked, pointing to Davenport's empty cup.

'Yes, ok, caramel latte please.'

Lambert ordered a black Americano and the latte. The parole officer twitched as he placed the cups on the table, and failed to meet Lambert's eyes as he sat down opposite him. Lambert was surprised the man was so nervous. Some of the toughest people he'd encountered worked as parole officers. It wasn't easy dealing with convicts and if Davenport acted this way with them he would be walked all over.

Tillman had never mentioned this side to the parole officer before. 'Everything ok?' he asked.

'Bit of a bad day actually,' said Davenport, finally making eye contact. 'Personal, you understand.'

Davenport looked unkempt. His shirt was crumpled and a day's worth of stubble was scattered around his face. If Lambert were to hazard a guess he would say the man was wearing yesterday's clothes and had spent the night away from home. He didn't indulge him with small talk. 'Glenn Tillman is missing.'

This got the man's attention. 'Jesus, I haven't heard about this.'

'It's not official and it's not to go any further than this.'

Davenport winced as he drank his latte, wiping a line of froth from his mouth with the palm of his hand. Twice he went to speak but held his tongue. 'I just can't believe this,' he said, finally.

'Tillman must have asked you before but how could Wyatt have staged this? He didn't have any money and was holed up in that cesspit of a halfway house.'

'I still don't believe he is responsible for killing your former colleagues. You learn to tell after a while in this business which of them are genuine. I thought Wyatt had put this all behind him. His counselling helped him understand why he'd acted the way he did, that it all stemmed from what happened to his mother. Remember, he'd still been relatively young when he'd killed those poor girls. He hadn't understood his actions then and I truly believe that by the time he'd left prison he'd come to terms with the enormity of what he'd done and why.'

'You weren't the only one fooled. The prison system, the parole board... Looks like Wyatt hoodwinked you all. You know who didn't believe him? Glenn Tillman.' Lambert drank his coffee, annoyed with his outburst but infuriated further by how this could have been prevented.

Wyatt was highly intelligent. He'd been studying economics at the University College London, having turned down an offer from Oxford. In prison he completed three degrees including his PhD. He'd been seen as a model prisoner who'd used his time inside constructively.

Davenport went on the defensive. 'I am sorry this has happened to your colleague, truly I am, and I hope you find him but I'm not sure what this has to do with me. Up until the day he disappeared, Wyatt had reported to our meetings on time. He'd managed to find work, his behaviour was exemplary. There is no way we could know what he was up to.'

'No one's blaming you. I'm looking for solutions. Where could he have taken Tillman?'

Davenport gave him a list of possible locations - the house where his mother lived before she died, the flat of a former jail mate in east London, his old university address - but these places had already been exhausted during the search for Devlin and Kirby.

'I need something new,' demanded Lambert. 'Had he developed any relationships since he'd left prison?'

'You have everything already. I truly am sorry,' said Davenport, getting to his feet.

Lambert controlled his temper as the parole officer walked away. If what had happened to Devlin and Kirby was anything to go by there was still a small possibility Tillman was alive somewhere, but already time was slipping by.

'Fuck,' he shouted, startling a young woman engrossed on her laptop as he remembered he had to pick up Chloe from the child-minder's today as Sophie had a work function. Fortunately he still had time. The childminder picked Chloe up from school and looked after her until 6pm. He caught first the tube then the train to Clock House, his mind still focused on the case. There was something he was missing, an anomaly that would prove to be obvious later in the case.

Chloe wore the same disgruntled look she wore every time he picked her up this late from the childminder's. It hadn't been so bad when she'd been in preschool, but now she was in primary school he felt guilty she had to attend the childminder's as well. Sophie was working towards a partnership at her city-based solicitors firm and with Lambert's unpredictable work patterns it was a wonder they managed to manage the child care as well as they did. As it was, they often had to rely on Sophie's mother to help out.

The tears started as soon as they left the house and began the short walk back to their house. 'I'm tired, carry me,' said Chloe.

'Come on, now, it's not that far,' said Lambert, trying not to take the day's concern's out on his daughter.

'I'm tired,' insisted Chloe, stopping dead still.

'You're too big to be carried, now, Chloe. You're in school.'

'I'm tired.'

The stand off lasted five minutes, Lambert ashamed at having to resort to bribery over dessert to get his daughter to move. Thankfully, her mood picked up when she was in the house and he'd fed her some beans on toast - the childminder provided her with dinner but the portions, and menu, didn't always suit Chloe's tastes. 'When's Mummy coming home?' she asked, once she'd finished, her mouth coated in orange sauce.

'Not until late,' said Lambert, replacing her plate with a bowl of ice cream. Although Chloe had been planned, neither Lambert nor Sophie had appreciated the full impact having a child would have on their lives. The first eighteen months had been manageable, Sophie receiving a generous maternity leave from her firm, but Sophie had been itching to get back to work within weeks of Chloe being born and had started taking on some work at home from month six. Numerous times, Lambert had considered leaving the force to spend more time with his family but as Sophie liked to point out to him, the police force was a part of him he would never be able to walk away from.

As Lambert put his daughter to bed, he thought about his old university friend, Billy Nolan, who'd been murdered in the halls of residence during their time at Bristol University. Lambert was self-aware enough to know that part of the reason for him joining the police was a never-ending search to atone for Billy's death, even though he'd been helpless to stop it. He lived with Billy's death on a daily basis, pictured the murder scene – the blood-splattered room, the empty sockets where his friend's eyes were removed, the Latin phrase, *In oculis animus habitat,* hacked into his flesh – every night before he fell to sleep.

And now, if Wyatt's timetable was reliable, he was six days away from experiencing that very same trauma. Remembering Devlin and Kirby's murder scenes, he pictured fishing Tillman's bloated corpse out of the Thames and swore to himself he wouldn't let it happen this time.

## 6

The silence was the worst part. Aside from the gentle hum of an electrical appliance somewhere behind him, Tillman couldn't make out any sounds that might give away his location. Tillman was never sure when Wyatt would strike. He tried to measure time but it was impossible in the darkness of the locked room. He was chained, hands behind his back, to metal railings. Still gagged, his clothes were damp from where Wyatt had water boarded him.

The thought of the torture made Tillman shake. He'd trained for such eventualities. First in the military, and latterly whilst heading up his specialised division of the SOCA, the Group. The Group was cross collaboration between the SOCA and MI5. They'd worked on hostage-taking scenarios during training, an ex-SAS operative managing the program. During that time, Tillman had spent over forty-eight hours, on three separate occasions, under simulated conditions. He'd been bound and tied like now, but then only a hood had been placed over his head depriving him of his sight. And although those times had been some of the hardest he'd ever experienced, pushing his sanity to the brink, at the back of his mind he'd always had the comfort of knowing it was training; that if he gave the word it would stop. He didn't have such luxury now, and he knew how this ended. He'd seen the bodies of his two old colleagues, Devlin and Kirby.

He'd had the chance to end this twenty-five years ago. Kirby had wanted Wyatt dead and Devlin, ever the helpful accomplice, had been willing to help him. At first they'd ignored Tillman's interjection, his threats that he wouldn't go along with their story. Kirby had said it would be his word against theirs but when Tillman cracked his baton against Devlin's lower back, the two men had soon understood his will out matched theirs. They'd left the force a few years later and Tillman hadn't seen them since that uneasy day in the bar during Wyatt's parole hearing, and then at their murder scenes.

Conflicting thoughts had occupied Tillman ever since his imprisonment. If he'd let Kirby and Devlin kill Wyatt all these years ago then they would still be alive but that wasn't what troubled him. It was his own silence. He'd done it to protect his friends, and to ensure that Wyatt was incarcerated with no difficulty. Had he made the right choice? One thing was for sure: their deaths would hang over him for the rest of his life, however short that might prove to be.

The door of his prison rattled, a gentle cold breeze billowing from outside as Wyatt, still masked, stepped inside and shone a torch directly into Tillman's eyes. Specks of light danced in front of Tillman's eyes as Wyatt moved towards him carrying a rag and a water container.

Tillman shifted, the cold metal of his cuffs tearing against his flesh as he tried to pull free from his restraints as Wyatt edged nearer. 'You don't need to do this, I can help you, Wyatt,' he said, pleased to hear some determination in his voice.

Wyatt paused before pulling his legs away and pinning him to the floor. Tillman's last thought as the rag was placed over his face was a silent prayer to Michael Lambert. He'd never told the man, probably never would, but he was one of the most astute officers he'd ever worked with. If anyone could get him out of this situation, it would be Lambert.

The thought disappeared as soon as it arrived, all sense leaving his mind as the water fell onto his face.

## 7

The front door clicked open sometime after midnight, Sophie returning from work. The noise woke Lambert from a fitful sleep and he listened to her move around the house, first upstairs to Chloe's room, then the bathroom, before joining him. She always tried her best to be quiet when she returned but never failed to wake him. 'What time do you call this?' he joked, as she crept into bed her cold feet touching his legs and making him jump. 'Jesus, you been out in the snow?'

'You shush up,' said Sophie, moving towards him and his body heat. 'I'm knackered. I need to be in for nine again. Can you take Chloe?'

'I'll have to drop her to the breakfast club again as I need to be in early as well.'

Lambert hadn't yet told her about Tillman. It would be an understatement to say she wasn't a fan of Lambert's superior. She liked to call him a throwback, an old-style bully and this was after meeting him on only a couple of occasions. Sophie had an unnerving knack of getting to the root of someone's personality but he'd always thought she'd misread Tillman. Yes, he was loud and obnoxious but Lambert had learnt to ignore some of his behaviour especially his over-zealous motivational talks. Sophie's opinion of Tillman was distorted as she heard about him only when Lambert was having a bad day. Tillman had another side, and the part Lambert admired the most was his loyalty. He was a leader and every one of his team knew the man would do anything to protect them. Lambert understood first-hand how difficult it was to manage the disparate members of the Group, especially the MI5 agents who initially hadn't taken kindly to being led by a SOCA officer. Tillman had succeeded in changing their minds and, in turn, he'd earned the unwavering loyalty of his team.

'Again?'

'I had to go in early this morning.'

'How did Chloe like that?'

'I'll think she'll forgive me in a few months,' said Lambert, as Sophie fell asleep.

Sleep didn't return so easily for Lambert, his mind playing the case over and over in his head until it stopped making sense. When he did fall asleep, his dreams were blighted by nightmares of drowning and the bloated images of Devlin and Kirby's corpses washed up on the shore.

It was a relief when daylight pierced the curtains of the bedroom. Sophie was already downstairs with a sleepy looking Chloe, who scowled at him as he entered the kitchen. 'And good morning to you,' said Lambert, kissing his daughter on the forehead.

'She doesn't want to go to the breakfast club,' said Sophie.

'It's horrible,' said Chloe.

'I'm sorry, Chloe, but I don't have any other option. I have some very important work on at the moment.'

Chloe grimaced before biting down on some toast.

'We should ask my Mum to come over if you're going to be busy,' said Sophie.

The insinuation was obvious– he'd promised to take Chloe to school all this week – but he refrained from getting into an argument. 'If you think she wouldn't mind. The next few days are going to be difficult for me,' he said, thinking about the time he had left to find Tillman.

Despite the early rise, he didn't reach the office until 8.30am. Adrienne was already there but didn't comment on his timekeeping. 'There's coffee,' she said, once he'd settled.

'Lifesaver,' said Lambert. The coffee was piping hot and flavourless. Lambert squirmed as he drank it, receiving a look of amusement from his colleague.

They updated each other on their work. Adrienne had spent the previous day exploring the previous crime scenes, working through the DNA records they had from the Devlin and Kirby crime scenes. Wyatt had been extremely careful. No traces had been found of him at either scene.

'The two scenes were less than a mile apart,' she said, telling Lambert something he already knew.

'We have search teams down there at the moment?'

'Yes.'

'What are we telling them?'

'That Wyatt may have struck again. No need for them to know about the boss just yet.'

'We may not have that luxury for much longer,' said Lambert, sharing details of his meeting with Hogg.

'He wouldn't be so stupid as to go public,' said Adrienne.

'Maybe not but we didn't leave on best terms. The four of

them had a strange relationship. I can't figure it out and as you know Tillman had never been one for talking.'

'Hogg was with you at the parole meeting?'

'You heard about that?'

Adrienne raised her eyebrows, highlighting the pointlessness of Lambert's question. 'Tillman told me during the Kirby investigation. Why hasn't Hogg printed anything on this story?'

'Claims it's a conflict of interest.'

Adrienne snorted. 'Like that's ever stopped anyone. The Chief has asked to see me this morning.'

Lambert agreed. Why had Hogg held onto the story all this time? Hogg had suggested he had respect for Tillman but Lambert doubted it extended that far, more likely Tillman had something on the journalist. He hoped he'd get the chance to ask him one day.

'Something I should know?' asked Lambert. Although the case was unofficial at the moment, Lambert was technically the Senior Investigating Officer. It didn't make sense that Adrienne would be the Chief's main contact.

'What can I say? I go back a long way with Hickman, though you wouldn't guess so if you considered my rank. He wants everything done on the quiet. Better you get on with what you do best, Michael.'

Lambert decided not to share Hogg's revelation about Devlin and Kirby attacking Wyatt. Although it was a potential motive for Wyatt's taking revenge, it was still just conjecture and he didn't want to sully Tillman's reputation on the hearsay of the journalist. 'Maybe suggest to his holiness that we get some more help on this. It seems pointless keeping this secret now. Hogg knows Glenn's missing so why can't everyone else?' said Lambert.

'I'll pass on your comments,' said Adrienne.

With nothing else to sustain him, Lambert poured another cup of the burnt coffee. At his desk, he scrolled through the old case files from Wyatt's initial murders through to the deaths of Kirby and Devlin. As the information played out on one of the computer screens, he used his laptop to download all the newspaper cuttings from Dan Hogg related to the old cases. Working this way made the information settle but it also helped him spot things he might otherwise miss; an occasional fact, or statement that appeared innocuous but could change the case.

After reading Hogg's reports, he uploaded Joseph Wyatt's case file. As his parole officer had stated, Wyatt was a gifted academic. Reports from his tutors at UCL, and his first-year exams, placed him in the top ten percentile in his year and it seemed that prison hadn't held him back. His subsequent degrees – undergraduate economics, masters in criminology, PhD in psychology - suggested he hadn't wasted his time inside, so why had he resumed killing the moment he'd been allowed out?

Lambert understood that killing was often a compulsion that couldn't be managed, yet he still found it hard to comprehend why Wyatt would move on to such obvious targets so soon after being released whatever his desire for revenge. He was extremely intelligent so why hadn't he tempered his compulsion, or at least focused it on different victims where he wouldn't be so obvious a suspect?

After he'd finished reading the files, Lambert went back to the beginning of the investigation. The first victim, Michelle Lewis had been discovered almost twenty-five years ago to this day. Lambert studied the grainy image of her lifeless body tangled in the vines and mud of the Thames. She'd

been on the same course as Alice Fowler, both members of
the rowing club at UCL. Lambert scrolled through Tillman's
case reports from that time, noting the contribution from the
criminal psychologist, Simon Travis. Travis predicted - once
Michelle and the second victim's cause of death was
confirmed as forced drowning - that the killer would have a
traumatic affinity with water from their childhood, the sole
clue that eventually led to Wyatt. The theory didn't seem to
be a great leap of logic and Lambert imagined Tillman had
probably been looking along those lines of investigation
anyway.

A newspaper article was in the appendix, predating
Michelle Lewis's death by fifteen years. It described the death
of Carla Wyatt from drowning. The woman had fallen into
the river when she'd been walking the five-year old Joseph
Wyatt. Unable to swim, and alone save for her young son,
she'd drowned.

Lambert scrolled for further records searching for the
exact location where Carla Wyatt had died and wasn't
surprised to discover it was only metres from where the body
of Michelle Lewis was found, by a stretch of river near
Putney. Using Google maps, Lambert found the area,
zooming in on a small building by the river's edge.

## 8

Any vague hope Lambert had that Tillman might be being held captive within the boathouse was dashed as he reached the grey brick building. The thick plastic boards which replaced the windows were immovable. Lambert checked the lettering: *Property of the Borough of Hammersmith and Fulham.* He walked the long abandoned jetty to the river edge. The wooden stands were rotten now and he would need to check if the building was abandoned after Michelle Lewis's death.

He made his way a hundred metres along the bank to where he estimated Carla Wyatt had fallen into the river. He tried to imagine what that must have been like for the young Joseph Wyatt, watching his mother drown whilst he stood helpless on the side. What must have those final seconds been like? His mother taking her final breath? Had she looked his way, pleading, before falling beneath the surface for one last time? How could a five-year old deal with seeing such a tragedy?

Unfortunately, Lambert had the answer to that. It was easy to feel sorry for Wyatt – and, to an extent, he did – but

only for the child Wyatt had been. Wyatt had killed those two
women without mercy – even if Michelle Lewis's death was
technically manslaughter - and had tried to do the same to
Alice Fowler. And now, all these years later, he'd started to
kill again. Lambert wished the boy's mother had never
slipped and fallen into the river, but nothing could excuse the
actions of the man Wyatt became.

Lambert returned to the boathouse and began playing
with the screws holding the boards in place. Although he
found it impossible to believe Tillman was here, he had to
see for himself. Ten minutes later, after having to explain his
presence to an elderly lady who was most perturbed by what
he was doing, he'd managed to make a hole big enough to fit
inside.

A paranoid part of him told him to call in his location, but
he dismissed the idea and climbed onto the edge of the opening. He shone his torch inside revealing a hollow, concrete
interior, and climbed inside. Cursing, as the material of his
trousers caught on a piece of jagged concrete sticking out
from the ledge, he landed off balance and toppled onto the
cold floor. His torch fell from his hand and for a short period
he was in near darkness. Lambert wasn't particularly claus-
trophobic, but the abandoned boathouse had a crypt-like feel
to it. He controlled his breathing as he retrieved his torch and
got to his feet. It would easy to talk himself into a panic but
he ignored the voice telling him to leave, and ventured
further into the building.

A musty, decrepit smell hit him as he moved through the
shell of the building, the build-up of trapped air. The records
showed the building had been used by the university rowing
team to store their equipment, but nothing here suggested
that was ever the case. A rotten wooden door, still signed with

a little man, led to a set of changing rooms. The toilets and showers had been gutted, the showerheads and urinals ripped from the white-tiled walls. Lambert stopped as a shadow flickered across the floor of the room, his torch alighting on the bloated figure of a rat scurrying into an opening at the base of the wall. Lambert released his held breath and moved faster than he'd have liked out of the room.

On the lookout for more rats, he entered the female changing room which was more complete than the male counterpart. Lambert opened one of the cubicles and was surprised to find a pool of stagnant water in the solitary toilet. He shone his torch over every inch of the interior but there was no sign of Tillman.

He tried not to hurry as he returned to the opening and refused to acknowledge his relief when he saw that no one had boarded up the window. He pulled himself onto the ledge, pleased to be out of the stifling building. Back in his car, he checked the day's itinerary prepared for him by Adrienne. Hopefully his next stop would shed some light on the abandoned boathouse.

ADRIENNE HAD CALLED AHEAD, so the Fowlers were expecting him. Lambert nodded to the two patrol officers situated outside the house. Mrs Fowler answered the door, shrinking into herself as Lambert showed her his warrant card. 'Please come in,' she said, as Lambert followed her through to a living room area.

The atmosphere in the room was reminiscent of that day at the Blue Boar pub, muted yet laced with the threat of potential violence. Alice Fowler sat on a worn cloth sofa, her body sunk so far back into the material it was as if she was trying to escape within its folds, while her father paced behind her ready to attack someone or something. Even the lighting reminded Lambert of the bar: dark and moody as if Mr Fowler had replaced the bulbs in the house with a lower wattage to match the family's dark mood. 'Another day, another copper,' said the man, as Lambert showed him his warrant card. 'I remember you,' he added, without looking at Lambert's credentials. 'One of Tillman's underlings.'

Lambert wasn't about to be dismissed or undermined by the man. 'DCI Michael Lambert,' he said, emphasising his rank.

'Get us some tea, Val,' said Mr Fowler, not bothering to ask Lambert if that was what he wanted. 'So how can we help you, DCI Lambert? I presume you're not here to tell us you've found the bastard.'

'Unfortunately not. I'm afraid Chief Superintendent Tillman has gone missing,' said Lambert, studying the flickering of emotion in Mr Fowler's eyes at the news as Alice sank further into her chair.

'I'm sorry to hear that,' said Mr Fowler.

Tillman had visited the house when Devlin and Kirby disappeared, had asked all the same questions Lambert was about to ask. The futility of continuing struck Lambert but he persevered. 'Obviously, you know what happened to Mr Devlin and Mr Kirby. Our hope is that Glenn is still alive and that we can find him before it's too late.'

Mr Fowler nodded and asked him to sit. Alice flinched as he sat down next to her. The woman was at least a decade older than him but she acted like a shy teenager, unable to meet his gaze. He recalled her in the bar, how she'd told her father about her witness statement. *I told them the impact he had our lives, Dad. On everyone's lives.* Lambert had long felt one of the deficiencies in his role as a police officer was victim support. Each day brought with it new cases, new challenges. It wasn't his role to focus on the ongoing lives of the many victims he dealt with. There was a necessary coldness needed in his role. He had to fight the risk of becoming involved during and after cases. If he did, he simply wouldn't be able to function. But with what happened to his friend Billy, he knew all too well the long-lasting impact crime had on people. And then he'd only been a bystander. Although very close to Billy, he was one of the many friends and acquaintances from university who'd had to live with what happened, who'd lived to survive another day. It was nothing compared with what Alice had gone through. She'd been seconds away from being Wyatt's third kill, though looking at her now Lambert understood she was just as much of a victim as the two unfortunate girls who'd lost their lives. She was broken beyond repair. She had a part-time job at a supermarket, probably no friends beyond the confines of this family home, and her parents weren't getting any younger. They too were victims. They'd lived to see their only daughter destroyed, the blossom of her youth stolen from her.

'Alice, I'm hoping you may be able to help me,' he said, softening his tone.

'How can I help you?' she replied, as though the request was an impossibility.

She recoiled as he told her about his visit to the abandoned boathouse.

'I think they stopped using it after what happened,' said Mr Fowler, taking a seat next to his daughter.

Lambert nodded. 'We think Chief Superintendent

Tillman might be being held prisoner somewhere. I don't want to get into the details but this is what happened to Mr Devlin and Mr Kirby. Can you think of any places where Wyatt could be holding him? Our best guess is that it would be near or next to the river. Is there anywhere you used to go with the rowing team, or perhaps on your own with Wyatt?'

A flicker of anger emerged on Alice's face, Lambert getting a glimpse into the character she once must have been. 'I was only alone with him the once,' she said, through gritted teeth.'

'DCI Lambert, I must insist. You're upsetting her. We've answered these questions a hundred times over,' said Mr Fowler, a protective arm placed around his daughter.

'Anywhere you can think of Alice, anywhere at all?'

'I've told you everything,' said Alice, not looking his way.

That much was true. They'd exhausted the search of every inch of the training ground used by the rowing team. Alice had always stated that the night of the attack was the first time she'd been alone with Wyatt and didn't appear to be changing her story. He was about to ask her one last time when out of nowhere, her mother burst into tears.

Lambert had forgotten the woman was in the room. Like Alice, she seemed to shrink into her surroundings. She'd been standing against the living room wall and now her legs gave way.

'See what you've done,' said Mr Fowler, rushing to his wife's aid.

Lambert stood. 'What's the matter, Mrs Fowler?' he asked, holding his ground as Mr Fowler comforted the stricken woman.

'He's going to come for her, isn't he?' said Mrs Fowler, her voice broken by uncontrollable sobs.

'No he is not,' said Mr Fowler, his words stern and author-itative.

'Your husband is right, Mrs Fowler. I don't think Wyatt will be coming for Alice and we have a team situated outside your house so he won't be able to get to you.'

Mr Fowler lifted his wife to his feet and with a sneer said, 'That didn't help your colleagues did it?

CHLOE'S GRANDMOTHER had already put his daughter to bed by the time Lambert reached home that evening. Thankfully, she didn't stay long and he was able to return to the case after ordering a takeaway dinner.

He'd met Adrienne after visiting the Fowler household. She'd spent the day coordinating a search of riverside proper-ties but the job was simply too big to hope for a positive result. Despite the Chief Constable's request, news of Till-man's disappearance had leaked, the Evening Standard running a front-page article on the case. Lambert saw it as a positive as they'd now been able to start using assistance from outside the Group.

Lambert considered the day's events. He regretted not pushing Alice Fowler further. He'd caved in too soon once her mother became hysterical and her father offensive. There was no talking to them by this point and he'd left his card with Alice and asked her to call him if she could think of anything further. He would need to speak to her again, ideally without her parents being present.

He'd finished the takeaway by the time Sophie returned home. He was reading through case files whilst a number of reports scrolled through the screen of his laptop. 'Sorry I'm late,' she said, bending over and kissing his cheek her breath light with the smell of alcohol. 'I'm going up. Need to be back in first thing. You coming?' she asked.

'Not just yet.'

Sophie offered a mock pout of her lips before leaving him to it.

His eyes were tired but, still, he continued reading. He'd gone through every file numerous times already, and had run searches on the System, the new database the Group were testing. He was out of ideas. The hard truth was that if Wyatt didn't want to be found, he wouldn't be. Tillman had thrown every resource into the disappearance of Devlin and Kirby so why would things be different this time?

Lambert swore and poured a glass of red wine from the bottle he'd opened but not touched earlier in the evening. It was an admission that the night's work was over. Once he'd started drinking, he wouldn't be able to concentrate. Despite its airing, the wine was acidic and not easy to drink. He took a second sip and tried one last search on the System. Although in its infancy, the database was connected to a number of organisations, including the prison where Wyatt had been held. Lambert ran a search on the prison staff. Tillman had already investigated every member of staff from the Governor down. He'd done the same for all of Wyatt's former cell mates, had even gone so far as to locate every prisoner to have been released since Wyatt's incarceration.

The second sip of wine was more palatable and a wave of heat overcame him. He clicked on one final button that listed the people who'd visited Wyatt at prison. It made for sad but interesting reading. In the last five years Wyatt had only ever received the one visitor: Daniel Hogg.

## 9

Lambert placed the glass down, his hand shaking, and reread the entry again. How in the hell had this been overlooked? Hogg had visited Wyatt fifteen times in the last four years of his sentence, the last visit only a month before his parole.

There was no time to wonder what that meant. He'd only had two swigs of the wine so was still able to drive. He found Hogg's address from the System and grabbed his car keys.

It was close to midnight, the roads pleasingly empty. He didn't call it in. It was too late to call Adrienne, and Hogg hadn't done anything illegal. If anything, the sensible thing would be turn back home and wait for the morning but Lambert was irked. One way or another, Hogg had lied to him. He claimed he wasn't writing a story on Wyatt so why had he visited him so often? It was clear the journalist knew much more than he'd let on earlier that day, and Lambert was going to drag every single detail from him.

Rarely had he made such fast progress through the city. The Blackwall Tunnel was all but empty and he reached Hogg's address in Barking within an hour. The journalist lived in a new-build cul-de-sac not far from the train station. It wasn't where Lambert had imagined Hogg would live and he realised he knew very little about the journalist, save for what he'd picked up during their two encounters. He was pleased to see the light on in Hogg's front room. Out of precaution – he had no way of knowing the extent of Hogg's relationship with Wyatt - he radioed in his location and knocked on the front door.

He was about to knock again when the door creaked open. Bleary eyed, Hogg squinted at him. 'Lambert?' he said, a lilt to his words Lambert hadn't heard before.

'The very same. May I come in?'

'What time is it?'

'Twelve fifty-five am.'

Hogg opened the door. He was wearing a thick maroon dressing gown, tied loosely across his torso. 'That late? You better come in.'

Lambert followed the man into the living room where the reason for the man's change in voice became evident. A half empty bottle of single malt sat on the mantelpiece, Hogg having already retrieved his glass. 'Get you one?' he slurred, swigging at the light gold liquid.

'I'm fine,' said Lambert, impatiently. 'We need to speak.'

'I'm here, aren't I?' said Hogg, unsteady on his feet.

'You should sit down. May I use your bathroom,' said Lambert, deciding a scan of Hogg's house was preferable to talking to him in this condition.

'You must think I was born yesterday,' said Hogg, clearly more drunk than Lambert had first anticipated. 'This is where you pretend to go to the toilet and find some incriminating evidence on me.'

Lambert tensed. 'Is there some incriminating evidence to be found, Mr Hogg?'

Hogg was thrown by the question. He swayed on the spot as he considered what Lambert had said, his face an ever-changing mask of comical gestures. 'Follow me,' he said, leaving the room and heading upstairs.

Despite Hogg's inebriated state, Lambert withdrew his baton not wanting to be taken by surprise. Hogg stopped at the top of the stairs, lurching backwards in a precarious fashion. Lambert skipped up and pressed his hand against the man's back to stop him falling. 'What do you want to show me?' he asked.

Hogg gestured to one of the two bedrooms. Lambert pushed him aside, his eyes never leaving him as he opened the door into what must have been Hogg's office.

Every inch of the room was covered in images and newspaper cuttings about Joseph Wyatt. Hundreds of yellow post-it notes covered the images. Lambert's hand went to his mouth. He turned towards Hogg for an explanation, but the reporter was no longer there.

## 10

The masked man – Wyatt – fed Tillman intermittently on dry bread and water. The irony wasn't lost. Tillman pleaded with the man every time he appeared in the makeshift prison, but not once did Wyatt speak to him.

Earlier – that day, yesterday, or minutes ago, Tillman couldn't tell – Tillman had spat out the bread force-fed into his mouth. Why, he wasn't sure - he was starving and his whole body craved sustenance. He kidded himself it was a way of proving he was still willing to fight, that he wouldn't be dictated to by the man. But he had enough self-awareness left to know it was a desperate attempt to end it. He was refusing to eat because he didn't want to survive, didn't want to endure another session of the waterboarding.

Although his eyes had adjusted to the darkness of his confinement, he still had no clue as to his whereabouts. His prison appeared to be little more than a wooden shed. Every time Wyatt opened the door, Tillman was offered a glimpse of the world outside and in. Naturally, Wyatt always came when it was dark outside, but Tillman still took the opportunity to assess his surroundings as best he could, in the distant hope that it could help him. The interior of his prison was lined with some form of insulation material to dampen the sound. The only noise he ever heard was the droning hum behind him. Through the door he would catch glimpses of the dark world outside: the silhouettes of trees looming in the night sky, the smell of compost and cut grass, and in the distance the faint sound of running water.

Tillman was too pragmatic to wait for rescue, but he was literally trapped. Wyatt had done a great job of securing him to a metal railing cemented into the floor of the prison. It didn't stop him trying to shake himself free, but the bursts of crazed energy where he fought his restraints took so much out of him that he'd stopped trying.

He was keeping sane by working through the exercises he'd been taught in training. The mental agility problems and recollections were helping him keep sane but still he twitched at the faintest sound, fearing Wyatt was returning.

It was inevitable that his mind would return to that day when he'd found Alice and arrested his captor. He wondered if Lambert knew yet the full extent of what had happened that day. The only other person alive that knew the full story was Hogg, and he'd proved to be a reliable keeper of the secret, despite his journalistic leanings – it helped that Tillman had something on the man, a drink-driving arrest Tillman had helped him with.

When Wyatt had taken Devlin's life, Tillman had understood immediately why, and he had known that Kirby would be next. Both men had tried to drown Wyatt and now he was out of prison he wanted his revenge. Tillman hadn't explained as much to Lambert and the team because even at that stage he'd believed they didn't need to know. It was

enough that Wyatt was taking revenge on the men who'd
arrested him. Only, that had proved to be an enormous oversight - an example of the arrogant way he sometimes
approached things. Maybe if he'd told Lambert the real
events from that time, all this could have been prevented.
He'd effectively saved Wyatt's life but he doubted the man
remembered as such. Tillman's memory itself was muddled.
He recalled the exertion of moving through the water, trying
to pull Devlin and Kirby off Wyatt while Alice was out cold
on the shore. As his two colleagues held Wyatt under the
water, he'd caught the death stare from Wyatt; his unblinking
eyes full of accusation as he struggled against his captives. A
day didn't go by when Tillman didn't wonder if that was what
had made him stop his two colleagues. It would have been so
easy to let Wyatt drown, and he understood his colleague's
desire to see the man die. Tillman liked to think he'd stopped
them out of a sense of righteousness, that he was upholding
the law he'd sworn to upheld, but if it hadn't been for Wyatt's
accusatory stare he feared he would have allowed the man to
drown.

And now? Now as the prison door creaked open, and the
masked figure of Wyatt walked into the darkness, all Tillman
could do was wish that he'd let Kirby and Devlin do as they'd
intended all those years ago.

## 11

Lambert found Hogg in the bathroom on his hands and knees, vomiting into the toilet basin. 'Now you know my dirty secret,' he said, turning to face Lambert, a line of sick still drooling from his mouth.

Lambert left the room as Hogg began retching again, unable to bear the smell of regurgitated whisky. What did this all mean? Was Hogg somehow working in cahoots with Wyatt? He would have dragged the man from the toilet and found an answer from him, but he was in no fit state to be questioned. Instead, he waited until Hogg had expelled the foreign bodies from his system and had sat up on the edge of the bath.

'I'm sorry you had to see that,' said Hogg, glancing at the toilet basin.

'*You* are?' said Lambert, moving towards the man and opening the bathroom window.

'After you told me about Glenn...well, I just went to pieces. I've been drinking since you left.'

Lambert returned to the bathroom door, blocking Hogg's exit. 'You need to explain yourself. Now.'

Hogg nodded, his eyes squinting shut. 'It started after that day at the bar. Wyatt's parole hearing. Those guys, they just pissed me off?'

'Devlin and Kirby?'

'And Glenn. The three of them were always so bloody righteous even at university. At least, they thought they were.'

'You were friends though?'

'If you could call it that. You saw the dynamics of our friendship that day. If we'd ever been friends, that changed the day Tillman told me what really happened with Wyatt.'

'I can understand that,' said Lambert.

'Maybe you can, but there was something I didn't divulge earlier today. I told you I never published anything about the incident because of my loyalty to Tillman and the other two but that isn't quite true.'

'Go on.'

'The truth is I was warned off. In the strongest way possible.'

Lambert tensed. The last thing he wanted to hear was that Tillman was bent, that he'd put pressure on Hogg to keep quiet. 'By Glenn?' he asked, knowing so much rested on the question.

'No. Glenn helped me out with a drink-driving thing. He thinks that's why I kept quiet – that, and the fact we were off record. Glenn is old-fashioned that way.'

'So what stopped you talking?'

'Aside from a lack of evidence? Devlin and Kirby paid me a visit and conducted their own little version of water torture on me.' Hogg broke down as he explained how the two policemen had used waterboarding techniques on him. 'Long before it became fashionable,' he said, wiping tears from his eyes.

'I'm sorry that happened to you but why the pictures of Wyatt in your room. Why the visits to the prison?'

'When you reach my age, Lambert, you start thinking back. You know, regrets. I knew Wyatt would be up for parole at some point and I got to thinking that it wasn't too late. That the world could know what really happened that night.'

'And what would that achieve?'

For a second, Hogg's demeanour changed. Gone was the pathetic creature perched on the edge of the bath. In its place Lambert glimpsed the resolution in the journalist, the anger that had driven him to this place. 'They tried to kill him, Lambert. Whatever Wyatt did, they shouldn't have taken the law into their own hands.'

'Did you kill them, Dan?'

Hogg did a double take. 'No, of course I bloody didn't. My plan was to write a story about Wyatt. I met Wyatt to find out what he remembered about that night.'

'You visited him ten times.'

'Yes, well that was as much a surprise to me as it is to you. I admit I visited him as a means to get back at Devlin and Kirby. I wanted Wyatt's version of events so I had back up for my story. I even tried to speak to Alice but she didn't want to speak to me. However, when I met him I stopped thinking so much about retribution. Wyatt is a fascinating person. I decided I wanted to write a book about him.'

'He's a cold-blooded murderer.'

'Yes, of course, I understand that. He destroyed so many lives and I believe he understands that.'

Lambert couldn't hide his incredulity. 'But what? You think he's changed?'

'He has changed. We all change, Lambert. I'm not the same person I was when I was twenty. Are you?'

'No, but I didn't murder two innocent girls and try to kill a third.'

'No one is excusing what he did. But there is more to it than that. He suffered a major trauma and no one knew how to deal with that. After his mother died he was put in care and suffered abuse, all the time having to deal with his mother's death. I don't think he meant to kill Michelle Lewis. He was obsessed with water and drowning. He held her under the water too long, and that experience did something to him.'

'You can't possibly believe that. Look at Lisa Bradford, what he tried to do to Alice Fowler.'

'His obsession overtook him. You must see that in your line of work all the time. But he changed in prison. He received counselling and began to understand his actions.'

'Jesus, he really did some number on you, Hogg. I thought you were a professional. What about Devlin and Kirby? If Wyatt is so rehabilitated, then why the hell did he torture and kill them.'

Hogg sighed. 'That's exactly my point. I don't believe he did.'

## 12

'Come on, Hogg, you can't really believe that?' said Lambert.

'I'm not stupid, DCI Lambert. I know how it sounds, and I know the lengths some convicts will go to avoid another second in prison, but I would stake my reputation on it. Wyatt has grown to understand what he'd done and why. His remorse was genuine. He had great plans for making amends when he was released.'

'Did you ever meet him outside prison?'

'Yes, on two occasions. He was settling into the halfway house and had begun volunteer work. I'd never seen him happier and then he disappeared.'

'Yes, three weeks before Devlin went missing. You must see how convenient that sounds.'

'I agree, but I swear it wasn't him.'

'Then who the hell was it?'

'You're the detective, Lambert. You tell me.'

Lambert called for backup and Hogg was taken into custody. There was no point officially interviewing him while

Hogg was still drunk so Lambert left the paperwork to the uniformed officers and returned home.

He managed to sneak into bed without disturbing Sophie but he was too restless to sleep. He kept thinking about Hogg and his relationship with Devlin, Kirby, and Tillman. Lambert didn't like to think of his superior as a bully. Yes, he was arrogant and forceful with his instructions and often gave the impression that he didn't listen to anyone but himself, but Lambert had accepted this as a result of his anti-quated management technique. Tillman wasn't above accepting confrontation, and occasionally advice. It was disappointing to think he'd kept the events of Wyatt's arrest to himself, but somehow more disappointing to think he'd had a part to play in the abuse of Hogg; someone he'd once called a friend.

The only saving grace was that Hogg had only accused Devin and Kirby of the waterboarding. Lambert hoped his instincts were correct, and that Tillman had no part to play in the journalist being warned off.

Hogg had sounded so convinced that Wyatt wasn't responsible for the deaths of Devlin and Kirby. Lambert didn't want to dismiss the journalist's theory out of hand, but his argument was flimsy at best. It was obvious he'd grown close to Wyatt during the times they'd met, and however much he might protest the chances were that Wyatt had manipulated him. How else to explain subsequent events? Perhaps once he was sober, Hogg would be able to take a more pragmatic view and offer them something worthwhile.

He must have managed to fall asleep as he was startled awake at six-thirty by Sophie's alarm. 'What time did you come to bed last night?' she asked, springing out of bed into her dressing gown as if she'd been awake for hours.

Lambert groaned. 'I had to pop out,' he said.

'Well, pop out of bed now and help me make breakfast.'

Lambert closed his eyes but he wasn't returning to sleep. He stumbled out of bed in a daze and headed downstairs where Sophie had a pot of coffee on the go.

'Lazy,' said Chloe, smiling as she played with one of her toys on the floor.

'I'll show you who's lazy,' said Lambert, picked her up and whirling her in the air.

'Not the best idea before breakfast,' said Sophie.

'Sorry, boss,' said Lambert, sharing a conspiratorial smile with Chloe as he placed her back on the ground.

He often took such moments for granted, but today he savoured the simple joy of breakfast with his family. Now he had a child of his own, he understood the cliché of children growing up too quickly. It seemed like only yesterday that Chloe was a babe in arms, and here she was now getting herself ready for school. Such things were inevitable, but sometimes he wanted nothing more than to quit work so he could spend more time with his daughter.

Lambert was surprised by the strange melancholy that crept over him as later he dropped Chloe at school. He presumed it was a response to the growing deadline on finding Tillman. It was still hard to believe his boss was missing. Lambert couldn't picture Tillman in captivity but he hoped that was where he was now. Better that than the alternative.

Adrienne had already set up the teams by the time Lambert reached headquarters. With the news out, the rest of the Group had been recalled and were doing everything in their powers to locate Tillman. By the time Lambert stood up to speak he'd already been taken aside by three of the team who'd complained about not being informed beforehand about Tillman's disappearance. Lambert passed the buck onto the Chief Constable but understood their concerns. If Wyatt was true to his past, then there were only five days until Tillman's body would be washed ashore, and in hindsight it made no sense that they'd not been informed.

Lambert told the team about his meeting with Hogg, ignoring the derision as he recounted Hogg's suggestion that Wyatt wasn't responsible. Hogg was still in custody and Lambert planned to speak to him again after the meeting.

Jeff Ballard, one of the SOCA officers, spoke. 'I don't like to jump to conclusions on anything, but all the evidence points to Wyatt. He disappears days before Devlin is murdered and the MO is identical. Wyatt is obviously manipulative, telling this journo what he wants to hear. And he did the same at that bloody parole hearing.'

Lambert agreed, but he also couldn't dismiss Hogg out of hand. In his inebriated state, the journalist had appeared so convinced Wyatt was innocent that Lambert was certain it hadn't been an act. 'I just want us to keep our options open. We need to focus on finding Wyatt.'

'The boss did exactly that when Wyatt first went missing. The man's disappeared,' said Ballard.

'We've got less than five days,' said Lambert, ending the meeting.

'Where are we at on the river property searches?' he asked Adrienne, at her desk.

'It's the proverbial needle in a haystack. There just aren't the resources or man hours available. Obviously, we've coordinated the searches outwards from the locations of where we discovered Devlin and Kirby but it's a mammoth job.'

'I'm going to speak to Hogg. Study his replies on video link.'

'Sir,' said Adrienne.

In the interview room, Hogg was wearing his hangover like a shroud. His shoulders were slumped so far towards the desk he sat behind that Lambert thought he was close to toppling over. When he looked up at Lambert, his eyes were bloodshot and his face pitted with dry scabs. 'Is all this necessary,' he said. 'Am I even under arrest?'

'I don't want to charge you with obstructing an ongoing investigation. Answer some questions and you can be on your way.'

Hogg tried to object but each movement appeared to be causing him pain. 'I've told you everything.'

'I need it on record and then you can go.'

Slowly, they replayed the conversation they'd had earlier that morning. Some of Hogg's words were still slurred, the alcohol yet to have left his body, but he repeated what he'd told Lambert. If anything, he was more adamant that they were chasing the wrong person.

Lambert studied the man. He was clearly telling his own version of the truth. 'Okay, you can go,' said Lambert. 'But I don't want to see any of this in print. Do I make myself clear?'

Hogg pushed himself to his feet, closing his eyes as if the exertion of standing pained him. 'I always liked Glenn. I hope you find him, Lambert,' he said, staggering out of the room.

## 13

After debriefing the team, Lambert headed to the local coffee shop to do some research free of the cloying atmosphere of the office. The rest of the team were just as incredulous about Hogg's assertion. Ever since he'd disappeared, everything had been focused on finding Wyatt. The rambling words of a journalist with a drinking problem were going to do little to persuade anyone that Wyatt wasn't seeking revenge.

As he was leaving the building, Lambert was stopped by a familiar face. 'Michael, I'm glad I caught you,' said the man.

'Sir, what brings you here?'

'Conference, you know how it is. I was told this morning about your boss going missing and thought I'd pay you visit. See if I can help in anyway.'

The man in question was Chief Superintendent Julian Hastings. Hastings was the reason Lambert was a police officer. He'd been the officer in charge of investigating Billy Nolan's murder and when Lambert had decided to pursue a career in the force, Hastings had given him tremendous support, advice, and, Lambert believed, a helping hand.

'That's very thoughtful. I could do with a quick coffee if you have a minute. I didn't have the best of nights.'

Hastings nodded. 'Show me the way.'

Lambert guided the man to a coffee shop close to the tube station. They walked in silence. Hastings had never been one for small talk. He walked stiffly next to Lambert. He was well over six foot tall, and looked even taller with his straight back and head held high. 'What can I get you, sir?' said Lambert, once they were in the shop.

'Just a coffee.'

Lambert returned a few minutes later with two black Americanos. He hadn't seen Hastings since his first year in the job though they talked occasionally on the phone. Hastings was of indeterminate age. He'd looked old when Lambert met him at university but looked no different now. He had the same angular features, the cold black eyes that matched the dry way he communicated. Although he'd helped Lambert considerably, he was not the sort of person Lambert wished to spend much time with. He was a stickler for rules and procedure and lacked anything in the way of a sense of humour. 'Thanks, Michael. So this business with your boss. Glenn isn't it, Chief Superintendent Tillman?'

'That's right.'

'We've met a couple of times before. Seems the decent sort.' Although Hastings meant to be kind, Lambert didn't fully believe him. He imagined Tillman wasn't his sort of officer at all. He was too brash, bull-headed and had a lack of respect for authority that made Lambert feel subservient.

Lambert told him as much about the case as he wanted to share. After he'd finished, Hastings sipped his coffee and remained silent. Lambert couldn't tell if he was deep in contemplation or was completely ignoring him. Eventually he said, 'Who has most to gain by Devlin, Kirby, and Tillman being dead?'

Lambert took his own time responding. 'Wyatt would have the satisfaction of seeing those who'd put him behind bars dead. Revenge is a powerful motive.'

'And the journalist?'

'Hogg? I'd concede his relationship with the man was strained but I can't see it. I suppose he could be using Wyatt's MO for effect and to take us off the trail but the man is a wreck. He couldn't pull this off.'

'You're probably right,' said Hastings, taking another swig of coffee before standing. 'Must get back to this damn conference,' he said, by way of explanation as he shook Lambert's hand.

'Well, it was good to see you again, sir.'

'You too, Michael. And please keep me informed regarding the case'

Lambert sat down and watched Hastings make his ponderous way out of the coffee shop and down the road. He wasn't totally surprised by the abruptness of the meeting - Hastings had always been a bit odd – but the encounter had been surreal and there had been a hint Hastings was withholding something. Hastings would be on first name terms with the Chief Constable and the doubting part of Lambert wondered if Hastings had been sent by Hickman to check up on him.

The meeting had made him think though. Of course, he'd already considered possible motives for Devlin and Kirby's murder, and Tillman's disappearance, but maybe they had been too focused on finding Wyatt. He'd seen similar things happen in other investigations. A reluctance to focus on other potential suspects when one appeared to be so obvious a culprit. Procedures were put in place to avoid this happening but it had happened. From the day Devlin went missing, all of Tillman's focus had been on finding Wyatt and nothing had changed since. Although Wyatt was by a mile the obvious choice, maybe it was time to look at other possible suspects. As Hastings had said, who had the most to gain by Kirby, Devlin, and Tillman being dead?

## 14

The question Hastings had posed still reverberated around Lambert's head as he returned to the office. It frustrated him that he still didn't have any answer beyond Wyatt. He poured himself some lukewarm coffee and took all his case files and laptop into an interview room so he could concentrate undisturbed.

He started with Wyatt's first victim, Michelle Lewis, and worked forward. The families of the two murder victims had been present at the bar on the day of Wyatt's parole hearing, along with the Fowlers. The three families had been close to indistinguishable. Each carried the burden of grief and loss, even though one of their number had survived the ordeal. No one wanted Wyatt released but that was no reason to harm Devlin, Kirby, or Tillman. The three men had been responsible for Wyatt's arrest. If any of the families had been out for revenge then surely they would target Wyatt himself, and if not him the Parole Board who'd decided he was free to return to society.

Still, Lambert read through all the details they had on the

family members. The surviving parents were all retired. Lambert could only imagine the pain of approaching old age with the grief of a dead child to contend with. He recalled the deathless stares of Mr and Mrs Lewis with their respective partners. He'd seen as much in Mr and Mrs Fowler and, though perhaps they should be grateful for the child that survived, they still grieved for the daughter they'd effectively lost that day – the woman Alice Fowler could have become.

Out of all the family members, only Lewis's younger brother seemed to have made something of a life for himself. He was a senior architect at a city firm, following in the path his sister would have taken. There had been so many people at the bar that day but Lambert remembered the man from his photo. He'd been well dressed, with perhaps an air of impatience about him. It can't have been easy for him either, living with his sister's loss and within the shadow of that death. Just the thought reemphasised to Lambert the greater tragedy of violent crime; the rippling effect it had through families and communities.

Trying to banish thoughts of Billy Nolan, Lambert turned to Devlin and Kirby. Both had left widows but neither had children. After leaving the force, Kirby had gone into security eventually starting up his own successful business whereas Devlin had moved into the pub trade working his way up to regional manager. There was little about their time in the police save for old case reports. Most of what Lambert knew from that time had come from Tillman, and was clouded by Hogg's subsequent revelation about the night of Wyatt's arrest. He searched through the old case notes, hoping for a hint about their characters, but couldn't find anything of relevance. It still made perfect sense that Wyatt would come after them, both for his incarceration and their attempt at his life.

Lambert slammed shut his laptop and swore out loud, receiving a startled look from a junior officer who'd been walking by the office door.

Was he wasting his time? All their efforts should be on locating Wyatt, so why was he bothering with all this stuff? He closed his eyes and sighed. Last night's lack of sleep was hitting him and he would have loved nothing more at that second then to fall on the floor and catch a few minutes respite. But there was no time for that. He returned to the files, knowing an answer possibly waited for him there. It wasn't instinct and he didn't believe in hunches. It was method. He'd worked this way countless times before. If there was a clue to Wyatt's, and hopefully Tillman's, location then he had to trust himself that he would find it. And the more he read and studied, the greater the chance of that happening. He had to ignore the other side of that fact, the argument that there was no clue waiting for him. It was a possibility he accepted but it wasn't something he could allow to derail him.

He rubbed his right hand across his face and picked up the notes he'd collected from Hogg's place. He'd made a cursory glance earlier and wished he'd looked closer. The transcripts from Hogg's interviews with Wyatt were fascinating. As the journalist had suggested, Wyatt was very intelligent. He talked eloquently on justice and psychology. When Hogg questioned him about the reasons for him being incarcerated, Wyatt didn't try to absolve himself from guilt. He admitted he'd done wrong and would forever be haunted by his actions. He'd planned to dedicate himself to helping victims of crime if he was ever allowed to leave prison.

Lambert imagined it was exactly what a Parole Board would love to hear and as much as he searched for a hole in

Wyatt's responses - a suggestion he was manipulating Hogg to his own end - he couldn't find one.

'I'm not the person I once was,' Wyatt had told Hogg. 'But that does not free me from what I have done. I understand that now. I don't expect the families to ever forgive me. But maybe one day I can give something back. Atone in some small part for my crimes.'

Lambert collated the transcripts, meaning to take them home that evening to reread. If Hogg was planning to write a book, he certainly had all the notes. Lambert searched through the other entries. There was little from the time of the original murders but looking through his notes, it looked as if Hogg had planned to speak to both Devlin and Kirby before they'd been killed. Tillman's name was also on the list, but that wasn't the name that stopped Lambert cold.

It was another name, someone Hogg had spoken to that made Lambert pack up his things immediately and leave the office.

The embryo of an idea grew as Lambert approached Hogg's flat. He needed to speak to the man again to find out why he hadn't mentioned the meeting in his notes. It could be innocuous but something about the way the meeting was entered in his diary suggested it had a greater significance.

Although Hogg wasn't under caution, Lambert had requested he go home and stay there, and the journalist had agreed. However, Lambert wasn't overly surprised when he didn't answer his door. He'd called him on his way over and each time the call had rung out. He tried him again and cursed under his breath as the phone kept ringing.

## 15

Every fibre of Tillman's being was on fire. The pain wasn't isolated. It coated him as if he'd been skinned alive and his nerves were exposed. A distant part of him– a part not retreating into itself, not overwhelmed by the tears which flowed from his eyes to meet the puddle of water at his feet – marvelled at how such an innocuous action could cause such catastrophic consequences. Armed with just a rag and a tub of water, Wyatt had inflicted a pain Tillman had never known; a pain he would do anything to end. As he flitted in and out of lucidity, Tillman conceded the pain was mainly psychological but that acceptance didn't help. He thought he was a hard man, perhaps not as tough as the personality he portrayed at work, but harder than most. His experience here had destroyed that illusion of himself. He couldn't quite remember if he'd begged the last time, asked Wyatt to put a bullet in his head, or if he'd fantasised that in the ensuing nightmares. Now he wished for nothing more than that sweet oblivion.

He cowed as the door creaked open once more. Surely he

couldn't be back already. It had been dark the last time he'd been here and it was dark now but time was an irrelevance. It could have been hours, it could have been days, since Wyatt had last been here.

Tillman's body reacted involuntarily as Wyatt approached. It slithered away from the man, pulling at the shackles holding it in place, while Tillman's mind welcomed the approach. Hopefully this was it. He didn't want to endure the torture again, but if it was to be the final time, if it would all be over, then he would welcome even that.

'Don't worry,' said Wyatt, speaking behind the muffled protection of his mask. 'We won't be doing that again just yet so you can relax.'

Tillman blinked, regaining his composure, ashamed by the tears still continued streaming from his eyes. Even in the extremis of despair, the detective side of him still searched for an opportunity. Wyatt had left the door open an inch and through the gap came the smell of burning wood, the distant noise of traffic. It gave Tillman a glimmer of hope and he didn't beg.

Sensing his attention was elsewhere, Wyatt looked behind him. 'My mistake,' he said, shutting the door and momentarily cloaking them both in darkness.

When he switched the torch on it was pointed directly at Tillman's eyes. Despite himself, Tillman let out a little yell of surprise.

'We need to wake up a bit, Mr Tillman. We have a lot to accomplish this evening.'

'It's not too late for you, Wyatt. Stop this now and I can help you.'

Wyatt chuckled and even beneath the mask Tillman thought the laugh sounded, if not familiar, then recognisable.

Wyatt lifted the beam of the torch over Tillman's head. 'He's behind you,' he whispered.

Tillman's breathing intensified as Wyatt moved closer. He wasn't carrying a bucket of water or rag but Tillman's body couldn't help but respond to his presence. It was all he could do not to scream as Wyatt moved passed him. Tillman turned his head at the sound of creaking wood and was surprised to see Wyatt pull at a hidden panel. With his neck crooked at a painful angle, Tillman watched Wyatt clamber through the opening and disappear within. The light vanished and for a second Tillman was swamped by the comfort of darkness, only for the torch beam to return as Wyatt pulled another panel clear to reveal a hidden door.

'Ex-builder you see. I started work on this a year ago when I suspected something might happen.'

Tillman turned away from the beam of light. 'What the hell are you talking about?' he asked, though subliminally he'd began to accept that he was facing a different narrative to the one he'd become stuck on.

'Here, let me,' said his captor, loosening the chain that linked his cuffs to the metal rod behind the chair. 'You can stand,' he said.

Tillman didn't know if he had the strength but wasn't about to let the man know that. He'd stretched his legs as best he'd could during his captivity, trying to keep his muscles in working order, but of late his willingness to do so had faltered. With his hands cuffed behind him, he attempted to push himself up from a squat position only to fall forwards. There was nothing to stop him and he hit the ground face first. Fortunately, the distance was not great and he escaped the fall without serious damage.

'Now that wasn't very gracious,' said the masked man, dropping the torch and dragging Tillman to his feet.

Tillman's legs were still unsteady and he was all but shoved through the opening where the source of the hum that had plagued him since day one was revealed.

The secret room was all but filled with an ancient deep chest freezer, and Tillman knew before the man opened it what he would find within.

## 16

Would Hogg have told anyone else about what happened all these years ago? Lambert hated indecision but he found himself standing outside the entrance to Hogg's flat, not sure what to do next. He had too little to take any action beyond tracking the journalist down. Anything else would feel like overkill, the work of a hunch and he didn't operate that way. He desperately needed to speak to Hogg but what if he was right? What if the entry in Hogg's notes changed everything? Despite the brittle information, he called Adrienne.

'Shall we put someone there?' she asked, not giving any indication to what she thought about Lambert's theory.

'You took the words out of my mouth, Adrienne.'

'I wish I hadn't answered now,' said Adrienne, already resigned to a night of sitting in her car.

'It shouldn't be for too long. Just keep an eye on the place. Once I've located Hogg I'll update you.'

'Sir,' she said, hanging up.

Decision made, Lambert began his search for Hogg. He started with the most likely place – the nearest pub. Unfortunately, Hogg's flat was only a short walk from a number of bars. Lambert trudged from one to the next. He had no photo of Hogg so had to rely on a description and a sweep of each place. In bar six on the Barking Road, The Boleyn, he got lucky. The landlady knew Hogg. Apparently he was a regular, but he hadn't been in all day. Lambert gave her his card but understood from the landlady's demeanour that she wouldn't be calling him if Hogg made an appearance.

Lambert made his way down Green Street, past the West Ham football ground. He half expected to see Hogg curled up in the corner of a side street, nursing a bottle of whisky. He'd obviously taken Tillman's disappearance badly. Maybe he'd felt the same way when Devlin and Kirby were killed. He may not have been on best terms with the men but they'd been to university together and had a shared history. And Lambert couldn't dismiss the other possibility: that Hogg felt guilty.

He saw him as he rounded the corner to the Red Lion pub. Hogg was leaving, surprisingly steady on his feet, and when he saw Lambert he stopped dead as if considering whether or not to run. As Lambert approached, Hogg's head fell to his chest. 'DCI Lambert,' he mumbled.

Lambert decided not to push Hogg as to why he hadn't answered his phone earlier. 'Dan, how are you feeling?'

'Fine,' said Hogg, lifting his head to make eye contact. Even in the gloom of early evening, Lambert could see the thin bloodlines snaking across the whiteness of Hogg's eyes. 'Listen, I know you said I should go straight to my flat, but I couldn't face being alone.'

'I understand. Shall we go back inside?' asked Lambert, too desperate for answers to endure a long walk back to Hogg's flat.

'I can think of nothing better,' said Hogg.

Inside, Lambert watched the journalist make his unsteady way to a corner booth as Lambert ordered the drinks – the weakest bitter he could find for Hogg, and a mineral water for himself.

Hogg grimaced as he took a swig of the red-brown liquid. 'What is this piss?'

'Probably more than you should be having. Have you been drinking ever since you left the station?'

Hogg shrugged his shoulders. 'What else am I going to do?'

'This has really hit you hard, hasn't it?'

Hogg took another sip, not grimacing this time. 'My relationship with Glenn is a strange one. We're not quite friends, not quite enemies. But I don't want anything to happen to him.'

'And the others?'

Hogg took another sip as if he had to drink between each utterance of breath. 'I didn't care for Devlin or Kirby. Not at University, not when they were officers, and not in later life. They were the wrong sort. Knew it then, and I know it now. However,' he added, pausing to finish his pint, 'I would not wish what happened to them on my worst enemy.' He lifted his empty glass towards Lambert, his eyes pleading for a refill.

'In a minute, Daniel, this is important.'

Hogg placed the glass on the table, and for one terrible moment Lambert thought he was about to cry. 'I've told you all I know, DCI Lambert.'

'The night when Alice was rescued. You said Glenn told you about that when he was drunk.'

'Pissed worse than I am now.'

'And he swore you to secrecy?'

'As much as a drunk man can. Lots of talk about being off the record.'

'But you told someone else, didn't you?'

'I told you, Lambert, but that was to save Tillman.'

'Not me,' said Lambert, raising his voice. He wanted Hogg to come clean, didn't want to force the story from him. 'Who else did you tell?'

'No one, I swear,' said Hogg, his face a mask of confusion.

'I've read through your notes. Think about it, Daniel.'

Hogg shook his head, searching for the memory. Then it appeared to come to him, his eyes widening as he considered the implications. 'I don't think that makes a difference,' he said shaking his head.

'Who did you talk to, Daniel?'

Hogg glanced at his empty glass, as if for moral support, and then told Lambert what he already knew.

## 17

Lambert called Adrienne as he made his way to the Fowler household. It was all conjecture at that moment but he needed other eyes there. The only other person Hogg had told about what had happened that night by the river had been Tom Fowler. On its own, that knowledge didn't mean much but Fowler had never mentioned it to Lambert and he needed to know why.

Adrienne confirmed she was stationed outside the house.

'Who have you seen entering and leaving?' asked Lambert.

Adrienne sighed, as if surveillance was beneath her. 'The daughter, Alice, arrived at the house thirty minutes ago. I presume from work. Aside from that, no comings or goings. Care to update me on why this is important?'

'Did you see anyone else in the house when she entered it?'

'No, but the light in the front room was switched on at five forty-five pm so someone else is at home.'

'Keep me updated,' said Lambert, hanging up.

The Fowler's house was only a couple of miles away in Poplar. A number of scenarios played through Lambert's mind as he approached the house. In an investigation such as this, there was always a danger of narrowing your options. The presumption all along had been that Wyatt was responsible for the murders of Devlin and Kirby. It was the logical conclusion. A released murderer, convicted for drowning two women, kills the two men responsible for his incarceration and kidnaps the third. It was even easier to make that assumption with the knowledge that Devlin and Kirby had also tried to kill Wyatt. But what if they'd been wrong all along? What if the killer was using Wyatt's past as a cover for their actions.

Lambert parked up next to Adrienne's car. A hint of ammonia hung in the air as he left his vehicle. Close by he heard the hum of the DLR, the overground track running close to the river. Adrienne wound her window down. 'Sir,' she said, slouched in the driver's seat as if she'd been there all day.

'Adrienne. I need to speak to the Fowlers. Secure the rear of the property.'

Adrienne straightened in her seat, pleased to see some action. 'Expecting a runner?' she asked, leaving the car.

'I'll update you when I've spoken to the Fowlers,' said Lambert, understanding Adrienne's desire for some answers.

Alice Fowler answered the door. She worked part-time in a local supermarket and was still wearing the uniform. She looked tired and withdrawn, older than she'd looked the other day. She stared at Lambert for a couple of seconds before she recognised him. 'Mr Lambert,' she said, unsure of herself.

'Hello Alice, how are you?'

Alice nodded as if that was an answer enough.

'Who's at the door?' came a shout from within the house.

'It's Mr Lambert, Mum. From the police.'

Lambert waited by the front door as Mrs Fowler joined her daughter. 'Well, don't let him stand there, invite him in,' she said, shaking her head at her daughter as she made eye contact with Lambert.

Alice blushed and pointed inside the house. 'Thank you, Alice,' said Lambert, following her mother inside. The interior was stifling hot, the smells of cooking – fried onion and fish – hanging in the air.

'Can I get you something to drink, Mr Lambert?' asked Mrs Fowler.

Thank you. A tea would be wonderful,' said Lambert, remembering the instant coffee he'd endured on his last visit to the house.

'Alice,' said Mrs Fowler, taking a seat on the flower-patterned sofa. 'Please,' she said to Lambert gesturing to an armchair next to the window.

Lambert's skin prickled with sweat as he took a seat, the armchair situated next to a radiator turned up to maximum. Neither Mrs Fowler nor Alice appeared to notice the cloying heat. Alice hovered as Lambert accepted a milky tea from her.

'Sit down, Alice. So how can I help, Mr Lambert?' said Mrs Fowler.

Lambert was surprised by the woman's confidence. On the previous occasions he'd met her, she'd been as timid as her daughter. Without Mr Fowler in the room, she'd taken over the role of head of family. 'I'm here to see Tom,' said Lambert. 'Mr Fowler.'

'I'm afraid he's not back yet.'

'Back from where?' asked Lambert, keeping his voice light and neutral.

Was there a flash of indecision in Mrs Fowler's response? Her hand went to cover her mouth as she thought about a response, a sign of potential deceit. Her eventual response was defensive. 'I'm not his keeper. He said he was going out earlier and he's not back yet.'

'So you don't know when he will be back?'

'No.'

'I see. Do you have a phone number for him?'

'I'm afraid he doesn't have one of those mobile things. We're not really cut out for modern gadgets.'

Sweat dripped from Lambert's brow. He couldn't understand how the two women could function in such an atmosphere. 'It is rather important, Mrs Fowler. Do you have any idea where we could locate him?'

'What's this about?'

Lambert paused. Had Fowler shared the information with his wife? That Devlin, Kirby, and Tillman had the chance to kill Wyatt but Tillman had stopped it happening. Would it have mattered? It was arguable that twenty-five years in prison was in itself a life sentence, though he doubted the Fowlers saw in that way. 'I really do need to see him,' said Lambert, with more force than before.

'I don't know what to tell you,' said Mrs Fowler, losing some of her earlier confidence.

'You must have an idea where he is. My colleague is missing, Mrs Fowler, I can't stress enough how important it is that I speak to Mr Fowler.'

The indecision on Mrs Fowler's face was evident. She would make a poor poker player. Her eyes twitched, her lips moving as if she was speaking to herself. 'He told me he would be back late,' she said, her resolve fading.

As she spoke, Lambert caught Alice's eye. The woman looked closer in age to her mother than the last time he'd visited. They could easily pass for sisters which was more a comment on the way Alice had aged rather than a compliment to her mother's youth. 'Alice, do you know where your father is?'

Alice glanced at her mother searching for permission. Mrs Fowler grimaced. With Lambert there she couldn't easily dismiss her daughter. He saw the hint of warning in her narrow eyes but Alice had already turned away.

'You could try his allotment,' she said, gazing downwards as if speaking to the carpet.

'His allotment?'

'Yes, he goes there all the time. Even more recently.'

'Where is his allotment, Alice?' said Lambert, heart racing and not only from the heat.

Alice glanced at her mother who appeared to be on the verge of tears. 'By the river,' she whispered.

## 18

'This is what you should have done,' said the man, showing Tillman the frozen corpse of Joseph Wyatt. 'Don't worry, I drowned him first.'

The light from the freezer shone on Wyatt's frosted skin, his face caught in a comical look of a surprise. 'Why don't you take your damn mask off now, Fowler,' said Tillman.

The masked figure nodded and Tom Fowler removed his mask. 'Very good, Chief Superintendent.'

'What the hell are you playing at Fowler?' said Tillman, taking some encouragement from Fowler revealing his identity. Now he could read the man's emotions, and could attempt to manipulate them to his will.

'I found out.' In the glow of the freezer light, and without his mask, Fowler looked his age. Tillman had experienced first hand the man's strength but there was a weariness to his eyes that suggested the killings had taken their toll.

'Found out what?'

'That night. When you found Alice.'

'What about it?'

'You had the chance to kill him. Wyatt.'

'Who the hell told you that?' said Tillman, his mind reaching for a drunken memory.

'Your journalist friend.'

*Hogg. Just perfect. What the hell happened to off the record?*
'Don't believe what you read in the papers, Fowler. You're old enough to know that.'

'You stopped them. Devlin and Kirby. They wanted to drown him and you stopped them.'

Tillman struggled in the chair. He didn't care what the man had endured, he had no right to take lives. He could understand his desire to kill Wyatt, but Devlin and Kirby? If he could get loose of the binds, he wouldn't hesitate handing out his own form of judgement on Fowler. 'I saved your daughter's life. Isn't that enough for you?'

'It's why I kept you for last but you should have let them do it, Tillman. You didn't save my daughter. Maybe if Wyatt had died she wouldn't be...like she is.'

'You still have a daughter, Fowler. You should be grateful for that. I'm sure the Lewises and Bradfords would change place with you without a second thought.'

'You don't understand, Tillman, how could you? He took her away that night and she never returned.'

'You think if we'd killed Wyatt all those years ago it would have made a difference?'

'We could have gone on with our lives knowing he was dead,' said Fowler, raising his voice. 'You have no idea what it's been like for us, watching our daughter slowly dissolve before our eyes and all in the knowledge that one day that monster would be released.'

Tears fell from Fowler's eyes, but Tillman had no sympathy for the man. 'If we'd killed him, all three of us would have ended up in jail and you wouldn't have seen justice for what Wyatt did.'

'Justice?' screamed Fowler, rushing towards Tillman. He thrust his forehead against Tillman's, spittle dripping from his mouth. 'They gave him an education and let him out. Alice never went back to university. She was left with nothing. No career, no future. She's scared of her own fucking shadow and you talk to me about justice?'

'You don't want to do this, Tom. I'm not to blame for what happened, I think you know that. You have Wyatt. It's over. I saved Alice, Tom. You won't be able to live with yourself if you kill me as well.'

'I don't intend to,' said Fowler, placing a hood over Tillman's head.

## 19

'Will you come with me, Alice?' asked Lambert.

'She's going nowhere' said Mrs Fowler.

Lambert had acted on instinct. He still couldn't believe Tom Fowler was involved with Tillman's disappearance. Although active and fit, the man was in his late sixties. Could he really have overpowered Tillman and the others? Retribution could be a driving force, but abducting the three men would not have been easy. 'Do you know what is going on here, Mrs Fowler?' asked Lambert.

'What do you mean?'

'I think you know. I think you both know. Is Mr Fowler keeping my colleague at the allotment?'

Mrs Fowler failed to meet his eyes. 'Don't be so stupid,' she mumbled, as if trying to convince herself.

'What has he told you?'

Mrs Fowler shook her head and began crying. 'Nothing, as always. He's been acting so strange these last few months but I can't believe he would do something like this.'

'He loves your daughter, doesn't he?' asked Lambert, causing Alice to stare at her mother.

'Of course he does. He loves her like nothing else, me included.'

'Don't say that, Mum,' said Alice, moving to her mother and tentatively placing an arm around her.

'It's true and it doesn't matter. We both love you Alice.' The words sounded forced and Lambert wondered when the last time her mother had said those words to Alice was.

'Then let her come with me. If anyone can stop your husband doing something stupid it will be her.'

Lambert called Adrienne and instructed her to wait with Mrs Fowler.

'What about back up?'

'Call for back up to come here but I don't want anyone going near the allotment and scaring Fowler off.'

Lambert was about to leave with Alice when she broke down. 'I can't,' she said.

'It's ok, Alice. I don't want to make you do anything you're not comfortable with.'

'I just can't. I'm sorry. I don't want to see.'

Alice began crying and Lambert understood Tom Fowler's anger. Twenty-five years on and still Alice couldn't escape what had happened to her. Wyatt had destroyed her life just as much as if he'd managed to kill her. 'Ok, Alice, you stay here with DS Corrigan.'

'My Dad will be ok, won't he?'

'I'll do my best to stop anyone else getting hurt, Alice, I promise.'

As Lambert made the short distance to Fowler's allotment, Lambert wondered how much Alice knew about her father and what she'd expected to see.

Mrs Fowler had given him a layout of the allotment fields that were much larger in scope than he'd anticipated. Lines of mini patches of field stretched into the distance, interspersed with the occasional building, everything clouded by the gloom of night. A small tarmac road divided two sides of the allotments but the main gate was locked shut so he couldn't drive inside. It was eight pm, the allotments deserted. A sign outside gave the name of emergency contact should anyone wish to gain access but Lambert had no time for that. He had two options: use bolt cutters to break the lock or scale the seven metre high fence. Although he had the necessary tools in the boot of his car, he chose the latter. If Fowler was somewhere inside, it would make it harder for him to escape and he didn't want to have to explain a broken lock, should his search prove fruitless.

The fence was sturdy enough to carry his weight. He threw his coat over the jagged top and hurtled over, his fingers gripping the other side of the fence as he dropped over. Lambert withdrew his baton as he made his way across the tarmac pathway. Fowler's allotment was situated to the rear of the site. Lambert shone his torch on the map Mrs Fowler had given him and tried to work out his bearings. He'd never seen the attraction of allotments before but as he walked the small incline he was taken in by the peace and isolation. It was like a little island of tranquillity and though he couldn't picture himself here – he'd never grown anything in his life, and was too restless to spend more than a few minutes on his own doing nothing – he could see how people could be drawn to such a place.

A movement to his left startled him, and he turned to see a fox. The animal was less than fifty metres away and stared at Lambert as if questioning his right to be there. The animal remained motionless as Lambert walked further up the incline before sprinting away into the undergrowth.

Fowler's allotment was at the far end of the fields. It was a secluded patch surrounded by a copse of trees. Low branches hung above the wooden shed at the end of the allotment that bordered the metal perimeter fence. Lambert shone his torch down the pathway, the beam of light dissecting the spot of land where Fowler had been growing various forms of greenery. Lambert edged closer. He couldn't see any sign of life within the hut but kept his baton withdrawn as he tried the locked door. There were no windows. The hut was encased by overgrown bushes that clung to the side and roof of the small building, the rear of the hut pushed tight against the metal fence so there was no other means of access. *If Fowler wasn't here where was he?*

He returned to the door and shook it a couple of times. He looked into the complete darkness and kicked hard into the lock. The door splintered but the lock held. He took a step back and tried again, the bottom half of the door coming way. A few more kicks and the door opened, a gust of stale air drifting towards him laced with something familiar but indefinable. 'DCI Lambert. Anyone there?'

His torch lit up the interior revealing a solitary metallic chair fixed to railings protruding from a concrete floor. Lambert edged nearer, his torch revealing a small watermark covering the base of the chair.

A humming noise came from the back of the hut. Lambert moved towards the noise, revealing a false wall with a small opening. He cracked open the gap and stepped through, his baton raised, before turning away as his torch fell on the frozen remains of Joseph Wyatt.

Wyatt's coffin was a deep chest freezer, the source of the

hum. His corpse was partially lit by the interior light of his coffin and his wide eyes stared at Lambert in perpetual shock.

Lambert had no time to concern himself with whether or not Wyatt deserved his frozen prison. The secret room held a back door. Lambert pulled it open revealing the perimeter fence, a section of which had been cut away. A piece of a clothing had caught on one of the rungs of metal. It flapped in the gentle breeze that carried the distant sound of the River Thames.

## 20

Tillman made it as hard as possible for Fowler, but he had so little strength left that it was difficult to fight as Fowler dragged him through the pathway at the rear of the shed. *Had Devlin and Kirby suffered the same indignity before Fowler drowned them?* He tried his best to question the man but the exertion of walking after his days of captivity left him breathless.

As the riverbank came into sight, Tillman collapsed to the ground. Neither Devlin nor Kirby's body had been found near to Fowler's house. He must have moved them afterwards and even in his predicament, Tillman scanned the night sky for sign of a vehicle.

Fowler didn't object to Tillman's enforced stop. His breathing was laboured and as Tillman lay in the damp grass, Fowler bent over on his hands and knees.

Once his breath was back, Tillman spoke. 'I saved Alice. Surely that's worth something to you?'

Fowler straightened himself up. 'But that's my point, Tillman. You didn't. You could have, but you didn't.'

Tillman sighed and sat up, the muscles in his arms tearing from the pain of being cuffed behind his back. 'He's gone now. You did what I couldn't,' said Tillman, changing tact.

'Yes he is, but Alice isn't back. She never will be. You have to pay for your mistakes, Tillman. I think deep down you know that.'

'For fuck's sake, Fowler. I have family. So did Devlin and Kirby. After all that happened to you, how can you do this? You will be destroying innocent lives, as much as your lives were destroyed by what happened to Alice.'

Fowler bent to his knees again, groaning from the effort. Tillman was surprised to see tears in the old man's eyes. 'Don't you think I know that? This isn't something I entered into lightly. I'm a fair man, Chief Superintendent Tillman. I know I have done wrong and I too must be punished. With Wyatt gone, and those who'd let him live punished, maybe Alice and her mother will be able to get on with their lives.'

'And what about you?' asked Tillman, playing for time.

For a split second, Fowler looked lost as if he'd not thought that far in advance. 'They'll be able to go on without me.'

'Think about it, Fowler. How do you think they'll feel visiting you in prison? They'll end up seeing you the same way you see Wyatt.'

Fowler didn't answer. He glanced towards the ground as if the answer lay in the soil beneath him.

Tillman understood. 'You plan to take your own life?'

Fowler nodded. He looked at Tillman, the glance almost apologetic. 'Yes, after I have taken yours.'

'You think Alice would want this?'

'Enough,' screamed Fowler, spittle flying from his mouth

and his face distorted into something Tillman couldn't recognise. 'On your feet.'

'Fuck you, Fowler. If you want me to go any further, then you're going to have to drag me there yourself.'

Fowler pushed Tillman onto his back, the force crushing Tillman's arms which were pinned beneath his weight. 'Let's see if you have the same resolve in a minute,' said Fowler, retrieving a cloth and a bottle of water from his rucksack.

Tillman did his best not to panic as Fowler placed the cloth over his face. He kicked his legs out to no effect as Fowler poured the water onto his covered face. Was this what insanity was like, thought Tillman as the panic took over every part of him. The feeling of his mind failing was tangible. He pictured it as a branch of a tree being snapped from the trunk. It was creaking, close to breaking completely when Fowler removed the rag. There was no relief in the sensation. Tillman choked and grasped for breath but however hard he fought he couldn't find enough air. He was lost to himself. A distant part of him heard Fowler talking, the sound of the night air billowing through the grass and the gentle trickle of the river, but Tillman was in a world of his own. His mind was a blank void, his consciousness stuck within the nothingness.

'Get up, Tillman,' said Fowler, shaking Tillman's limp and inactive body. 'You want to go through that again?'

Tillman stared blankly ahead as the words seeped through to the void. His reaction was visceral. At that moment he didn't understand what was being said, only the inherent threat. He stood up and allowed Fowler to guide him to the river.

## 21

Lambert crawled through the opening at the back of the shed, his hands and knees finding the murkiness of a cold puddle of water. Metres ahead, the drooping vines and trees gave way to a narrow pathway where he was able to stand. His torch revealed two sets of footprints and he began to jog, keeping his pace steady, refusing to panic, as he followed the dirt track towards the river.

He refused to think the worst. He had to believe Tillman was alive, and that he could reach him in time.

Once Lambert made sight of the riverbank he upped his pace, within seconds falling over an object in the middle of the track.

He landed heavy, his right knee striking a loose rock. The pain rattled through his body and it was a few seconds before he had the strength to check for damage. A second wave of pain caused him to close his eyes, as he stood and placed weight on the damaged knee.

The object was a rucksack filled with two large plastic containers full of water. Next to the bag was a third empty container and a wet rag. It was easy enough to deduce what had happened. The grass to the side of the path was flattened and it appeared some form of struggle had taken place but there was still no sign of Tillman.

The pain in his knee was still intense. In any other circumstances, he would have fallen back to the ground but the thought of Tillman forced him onwards. He limped forwards, hopping through the undergrowth until his knee started to accept his full weight again. He could hear the river in the distance cutting the quietness of the still night and all of a sudden he was descending down a steep incline. He slipped, his injured leg giving away, and stumbled down the hill using his hands and stronger leg to keep himself upright.

The river was in view now. It merged into the darkness of the night but he could make out its blurred meandering shape and the shadowy outline of two figures embraced as if lovers on the water edge.

ALTHOUGH TILLMAN'S senses had returned, he was not the same person. He'd been forced to change to save himself. He was surviving on animal instinct and understood there was only one way he would endure the next few minutes.

Fowler wanted to die. He'd admitted as much to Tillman in his pathetic attempt to justify his own actions. Tillman didn't know if he planned to drown himself afterwards – the very thought sounded preposterous – but he would be happy to help the man reach his goal. As they stopped by the water's edge, Tillman didn't waste any more energy reasoning with the man. He'd given Fowler that opportunity and it was clear he was now beyond logic. He would only have the one opportunity. His strength and energy were all but depleted but he wouldn't give in without one last effort.

'This is it then, Glenn,' said Fowler. 'Any last words?'

Tillman poised himself. His hands were cuffed behind him but he could still do damage with his body. 'Fuck you, Fowler.'

Fowler sighed as if disappointed. 'It will be so much easier if you don't struggle,' he said, grabbing the metal cuffs on Tillman's wrists with one hand as the other guided him into the water.

Tillman's heart raged as the cold water seeped up his legs. This can't be it, he said to himself. He stumbled forwards, allowing the water to reach his waist, and stopped dead and lowered his back. Fowler followed him, stumbling forward. Tillman used the man's momentum to flip him over his back and into the water.

As Fowler emerged, his breathless face a parody of the suffering he'd inflicted on his victims, Tillman lent forward and sent his head crashing into his nose.

Fowler fell backwards into the water once more. Tillman, who'd lost his balance, landed on top of the man. He began to panic. Being submerged was too reminiscent of his recent struggles. He thrashed in the shallow water as beneath him, Fowler slipped away.

Once more, Tillman's sanity was fading when he felt a pair of hands grip his handcuffs and roughly pull his head from the water. The cold air pinched his skin and for a split second he was back in the shed, sitting on the chair as Fowler removed the cloth from his face. He gasped at the cold air, only able to stand upright thanks to the man holding him in place.

Fowler didn't bother turning him around to face him.

Like Tillman he was breathless and it was some time before he spoke. 'Okay, shall we try that again?' he said, pushing Tillman back beneath the water.

LAMBERT TRIPPED down the hill as the figures disappeared from sight. As a child, Lambert had a recurring nightmare where he was trying to run to his parents' bedroom but an invisible force held up back. He was reminded of that now as he made slow progress towards the river. His knee throbbed and each step sent shivers of pain up his leg and spine. As the two figures resurfaced, he almost lost his footing again. He went to call out Tillman's name only to hold his breath as he saw the taller of two figures hold the other beneath the water.

Baton in one hand Lambert rushed into the water, the cold chill numbing the pain in his leg. Only the moon and the residual light from the distant city buildings lighted the scene, but he could see it was Fowler holding Tillman beneath the water. He didn't hesitate or call out either man's name as he swung the baton hard onto the back of Fowler's skull.

Fowler paused - as if deciding the effect of the impact - before falling forwards into the river. However, he wasn't out cold. His hands and arms braced for his fall, and as he landed he used the body beneath the water for leverage.

Lambert stumbled forward and grabbed Fowler by the throat. He was strong and it took all of Lambert's effort to drag him off Tillman. As he held him, one arm around his throat, Tillman emerged from the river.

Or what once must have been Tillman. In his place was a lost-looking character who appeared to have shed a quarter of his body weight in the four days he'd been missing. 'Glenn?' said Lambert.

Tillman nodded. 'I'm okay, Michael,' he said, sounding anything but. 'You better turn around though.'

With his grip iron clad on Fowler, Lambert turned around.

On the riverbank stood Mrs Fowler. In her hands, a loaded shotgun.

## 22

Lambert held onto Mr Fowler. The strength in the man's body had dissipated. He was now a bag of bones and it was taking all of Lambert's strength to keep him upright. 'It's over, Mrs Fowler,' he said as he stepped forward, Tillman keeping behind the shelter of the entwined bodies.

'You should have let him die,' said Mrs Fowler.

Lambert stopped moving. Fowler was still an effective shield against the gun but he wasn't sure how much longer he could hold onto to him. Fowler's breathing was shallow and he appeared to have slipped into unconsciousness. 'Your husband needs assistance, Mrs Fowler. Put the gun down and I will get some help.'

'Send out Tillman first.'

'I can't do that.'

'Then I'll shoot through you.'

'You risk killing your husband.'

Mrs Fowler laughed, the sound mirthless and unnerving. 'Don't you think I know that? He was going to die tonight anyway. We both were,' she added, lifting the gun.

'Why?' said Lambert, lifting Fowler as a shield and preparing to run towards her.

'It's over. Wyatt is gone, and those responsible have paid the price.'

'And what about Alice?' asked Lambert, his focus now intent on Mrs Fowler.

'Do you have any idea what it's been like for us with that girl? We've tried our best, heaven knows, but Wyatt killed her that day. Maybe if your boss hadn't been such a coward then this would have never happened. If Wyatt had been killed, then Alice would never have had anything to worry about?'

'Mum?'

Lambert had noticed the figure of Alice Fowler hovering on the hill behind her mother as soon as he turned to face the gun. As Mrs Fowler turned towards her daughter, Lambert dropped Tom Fowler and ran.

The river was a natural barrier and Lambert felt he was making little progress as he battled against the current. Mrs Fowler still had her back to him as he left the water, his feet unsteady on the slick mud of the riverbank. He wished she didn't have the gun still held in her arms. He had no idea if she'd used it before, if the gun had a safety button, or if her finger was on the trigger, but he didn't have an option. She had to be disarmed, so he ran straight at her legs like an over-enthusiastic rugby player.

She hadn't even hit the ground before the shot rang out in the still night air.

MRS FOWLER DROPPED the gun and lay prone on the floor as if the bullet had somehow hit her. Lambert secured the weapon before doing anything else, discharging the remaining bullet. His ears were ringing as he rolled off Mrs Fowler's body and stared at the space where Alice had been standing.

Lambert closed his eyes for a split second, preparing for what he was about to see. Alice lay on the ground in perfect imitation of her mother. He rushed towards to her, the shot gun in his hand, hoping instinct had driven her to the floor. 'Alice?' he said, scrambling to his knees and checking for her pulse and signs of an entry wound.

The woman opened her eyes and despite the circumstances offered him a smile. 'I think I'm okay,' she said.

As Lambert checked her over he turned his attention back to the river. 'Jesus Christ,' he muttered to himself. He would have laughed if he had the energy. Mr Fowler was on his back, his face facing the night sky, and was being dragged deeper into the water by Tillman.

Lambert sighed. 'Wait here, Alice,' he said.

'Glenn, what the hell are you doing?' he asked his boss, once he reached the shore.

'Leave it, Lambert,' said Tillman.

Lambert walked forward. Somehow the water was colder this time round. 'Just bring him back to shore, Glenn. I've had enough drama for today.'

'You don't know what he did to me?' said Tillman.

Lambert kept moving forwards. He hated the look of fear on Tillman's face. 'Glenn, you would never live with yourself if you did anything to him. I know he deserves it but you're not like that. You're not Devlin or Kirby. You saved Alice. Even saved that asshole Wyatt. You can't give it all away on Fowler. He'll get what's coming to him.'

'Maybe,' said Tillman, floundering.

They stood, staring at each other as the water flowed over

the still body of Mr Fowler. It was Tillman who eventually broke the impasse. 'You going to shoot me if I don't let him go, Michael?' he said, glancing towards the gun.

With that it was over. Lambert smiled. 'Something like that. Come on, boss, let's get out of this bloody water.'

## 23

'I quite like this,' said Chloe.

'Me too,' said Lambert, surprised his daughter had taken the words out of his mouth. They were making the short walk back from school together hand in hand and he'd just that second been thinking that life didn't really get any better than this.

Sophie was waiting for them at home. She'd taken a half-day off work and had prepared an early meal for them as Lambert had to head back into town that afternoon. In Chloe's honour, Sophie had prepared their daughter's favourite meal: breaded fish, chips, and peas with an endless supply of tomato ketchup.

Lambert thought it was possibly the greatest meal he'd ever tasted. He couldn't keep the smile off his face as he spoke to Chloe. 'I think you missed a bit,' he said, pointing to his daughter's face that was smothered in red sauce.

Sophie laughed and handed her a napkin. Chloe wiped her mouth succeeding only in spreading the mess further up her face.

It was difficult to leave. After the fallout from the Fowler case, the normality of home life had become even more attractive. There was nothing more he would rather do at that moment then spend the rest of the afternoon and early evening with his wife and daughter. He only had to make the short commute into central London, and would be back later that evening but, kissing Chloe goodbye on the doorstep, he felt as if he was going away for months.

The walk to Clock House station was painful. He'd gone through a course of painkillers for his knee but still felt a twinge every time he applied full pressure. His other leg was suffering now as he was over-compensating, and he promised himself he would book a physiotherapist appointment for later that week.

Ninety minutes later, he was at the Group's Headquarters. It was Tillman's first day back since the Fowler arrests and he'd requested Lambert meet with him at the end of the day.

The rest of the team were busy in the outer office. The Fowler case was more or less in the past now and they were working on more important projects safe in the knowledge that Tillman was back with them. 'I thought you were on a half day,' said Adrienne, looking up from her desk.

'His highness requested my presence,' said Lambert.

'He's only been back a day. What have you done now?'

'He lives to torment me,' said Lambert.

'It's thanks to you he lives at all.'

Lambert nodded and moved towards Tillman's office. Tom and Valerie Fowler were in custody following the events by the river. Tom Fowler had confessed to the murders of Devlin, Kirby, and Wyatt. He would most likely be spending the rest of his life behind bars. Tom Fowler's statement had included allegations about Devlin and Kirby attacking Wyatt all those years ago. Tillman had been questioned over the incident, as had Hogg. It was all conjecture. Tillman was the only survivor from that night and wasn't about to place himself in trouble. One day he might share exactly what had happened with Lambert, but that wasn't going to happen any day soon.

Valerie Fowler had been charged with conspiracy to murder as well as possession and use of an illegal firearm. The outcome of her case was less clear-cut. Her husband denied she had any part to play in the murders and she was refusing to confess despite what she'd told Lambert that night. Both were on suicide watch and would remain so for some time.

It was Alice Fowler who was of greater concern to Lambert. For the first time in her life, she was living without the support of her parents. She'd been appointed a counsellor and despite what happened by the river, Lambert had visited her on a number of occasions. He'd been surprised by the change in the woman. He didn't know if it was the death of Wyatt, or the incarceration of her parents, but she appeared to be not only surviving but thriving on her own. There was a lightness to her and she looked years younger. With Lambert's assistance, she'd enrolled on a pathway course at a UCL as a prelude to starting a degree. Lambert hoped she could now put her life together and maybe fulfil some of the promise Wyatt had taken from her.

'You wanted to see me, sir?' said Lambert, taking a seat opposite his boss.

Tillman smirked but there was little humour in the gesture. Lambert had to admit he looked good. The weight he'd lost took a couple of years off him and from a cursory glance it was hard to believe he'd even been held captive. Yet, a closer look at his narrow grey eyes revealed a change to the man. Tillman would never reveal to him what he was thinking, or the psychological impact his incarceration had on him. He'd shared the details of the waterboarding and it was a miracle he'd survived mentally at all. Tillman hated to demonstrate weakness and no doubt considered his abduction a failure. His eyes suggested a hardening to a personality that was already granite strong. 'Take a seat, why don't you,' said Tillman.

Lambert smiled at the sarcasm. Both of them had avoided one aspect of that night by the river. During interrogation, Tom Fowler had made some overtures that Tillman had tried to kill him and although it would be brought up in court, the fact that Tillman had been cuffed and led to the river meant that it was unlikely any jury would listen to Fowler's plea. Mrs Fowler and Alice had different recollections of the events and neither had backed up Mr Fowler's story.

Tillman grimaced and for one awful second, Lambert thought he was about to cry. 'I just wanted to thank you,' he said.

Lambert was almost as surprised by the gratitude as he would have been had Tillman had started to cry.

'You were right to stop me. I wasn't thinking straight at that time. You know what he did to me...'

'You don't need to defend yourself to me, Glenn.'

Lambert had already come to terms with what had happened. In his report, Lambert had included everything that had happened that night. It was a question of context. He'd described Tillman's attack on Fowler as a further altercation between the pair which to a certain extent was the truth. He couldn't be sure as to Tillman's intent and saw no point offering an opinion. Fowler was still alive and Lambert saw no need for Tillman's career to suffer for the sake of a murderer who'd forced him to endure days of torture.

As for what had happened on the night Tillman rescued Alice Fowler, that was one for his boss's conscience. Lambert had no doubt that Tillman had done the right thing stopping Devlin and Kirby killing Wyatt. He couldn't say the same about Tillman's ensuing silence. Devlin and Kirby had left the force shortly afterwards and Wyatt had correctly been incarcerated. Tillman had no way of knowing if speaking up sooner would have stopped Fowler killing his victims. He wished Tillman had told him about it sooner but was prepared to give his boss the benefit of the doubt. In his own twisted way, he'd still been protecting Devlin and Kirby's reputation and Lambert admired his sense of loyalty, however ill-judged.

Tillman nodded as if his thoughts had been matching Lambert's. 'Either way, Michael, I appreciate what you did for me. I won't forget it.'

'I feel like we're in a movie, here Glenn,' said Lambert, trying to make light of the conversation. 'Next you'll be telling me you owe me a favour.'

Tillman narrowed his eyes, and tilted his head to the side.

They never spoke directly about either night again.

# PREVIEW OF DEAD EYED (DCI LAMBERT 1)

If you've enjoyed Dead Water, please take a couple of moments and leave a review. Each review makes such a difference to the visibility of the book online and is hugely appreciated by everyone involved in the production of the book...

Now, keep reading for a sneak peek of DCI Lambert book 1, Dead Eyed...

# DEAD EYED

## Prologue

The man hovered on the edge of the dance floor. His elongated limbs and thinning hair made him stand out from the young lithe bodies. Sam Burnham watched him from the bar, nursing the same brandy he'd ordered an hour ago.

The track ended and the man shuffled his feet. He scanned the mirrored dance area before heading towards the bar.

Burnham ordered a second drink. He sensed the man in his periphery, and turned to face him. He placed his hand on the younger man's arm, and looked him directly in the eyes.

'Can I buy you a drink?' he asked.

The man nodded, staring at Burnham. Twenty minutes later they left the club together.

'What now?' asked Burnham, pulling his jacket tight against his body. It was a late September evening in Bristol, and the temperature had dropped since he'd set out earlier that day.

'Where are you staying?' asked the man. His eyes darted in random directions, not once focusing on Burnham.

'Hotel. You wouldn't like it. Do you live near?' Burnham knew exactly where he lived.

'I'm not sure,' said the man. 'I don't know you.'

Burnham touched the man's arm again. It was the simplest of techniques, but highly effective.

The man relented. 'It's not far away. We can walk.'

The man lived in Southville, a small suburb of Bristol less than a mile from the centre. They walked in an awkward silence, peppered with the occasional question from the man.

The man stopped outside a block of flats. 'I don't mean to sound weird, but do I know you from somewhere?'

'I don't think so. I guess I must have one of those faces,' said Burnham, following him inside.

The flat was hospital clean, the air fragranced artificially. The living area was an array of various gleaming surfaces: glass, chrome, marble. Burnham accepted a glass of brandy. The man's hands trembled as he handed it over.

They moved to the living room sofa and the man made life easy for him. 'I'll be back in a minute,' he said, his voice faltering.

As soon as Burnham heard the bathroom door click shut, he removed the phial from his inside jacket pocket. He broke the seal and spilled the clear liquid into the man's drink, stirring it with his left index finger.

It took five minutes for the man to take a drink. A further five minutes for the drug to take effect. Burnham dragged him to the bedroom, the man's skeletal body insubstantial in his thick arms. He placed the man on the bed and made a phone call.

Burnham's boss arrived at the flat two minutes later

carrying a small leather case. Burnham watched in silence as he removed a surgical outfit, a set of scalpels, and a second phial filled with a different substance. 'Wait in the car,' he ordered.

It was three hours before his boss left the building. Burnham hurried from his seat and opened the back passenger door for him.

'Do you need me to clean up?' he asked.

'No, not this time.'

# CHAPTER ONE

Michael Lambert waited at the back of the coffee shop. To his right, a group of new mothers congregated around three wooden tables. Some held their tiny offspring; the others allowed their babies to sleep in the oversized prams which crowded the area. Two tables down, a pair of men dressed in identical suits stared at their iPads. Next to them, a young woman with braided hair read a paperback novel. All of them looked up as Simon Klatzky walked through the shop entrance and shouted over at him.

Lambert ignored the glances. He'd arrived thirty minutes earlier, out of habit checking and rechecking the clientele. He hadn't noticed anything out of the ordinary. He stood and beckoned Klatzky over. He'd last seen him two years ago at the funeral. 'Good to see you again, Simon,' he said.

'Mikey,' said Klatzky. Like Lambert, Klatzky was thirty-eight. He'd lost weight since the last time they'd met. His face was gaunt, his eyeballs laced with thin shards of red. When he spoke, Lambert noticed a number of missing teeth. The rest were discoloured and black with cheap fillings. His face cracked into a smile. He stood grinning at Lambert. In his left hand he clutched an A4 manila envelope.

'Sit down then. What do you want to drink?' said Lambert.

Klatzky shrugged. 'Coffee?'

Lambert ordered two black Americanos and returned to the table.

'Sorry I'm late,' said Klatzky.

Klatzky had called earlier that morning desperate to meet. He'd refused to tell Lambert the details over the phone but had insisted that it was urgent. From the smell of him, it hadn't been important enough to stop him visiting a bar first.

Klatzky's hands shook as he sipped the coffee. 'I thought it best you see for yourself,' he said, looking at the envelope still clutched tight in his hand.

Lambert sat straight in his chair, scratching a day's growth of stubble on his face. It was genuinely good to see his old friend. He'd only agreed to meet him as he'd sounded so scared on the phone. Now he was here, Lambert regretted not seeing more of him in the last two years.

'How have you been, Si?'

'So-so. I'm sorry I haven't called before.' He hesitated. 'And now, contacting you in these circumstances.' He still had a strong grip on the envelope, his knuckles turning white with the effort.

'I'm not working at the moment, Simon.'

'I didn't know who else to talk to.' Klatzky produced a bottle of clear liquid from his grainy-black rain jacket and poured half the contents into his coffee cup.

Some things didn't change. 'Are you going to show me then?' Lambert didn't want to rush him, but he didn't like surprises. He needed to know what Klatzky wanted.

Klatzky drank heavily from the alcohol-fused drink, momentarily confused.

'The envelope, Si.'

Klatzky stared at the envelope as if it had just appeared in his hand. He handed it to Lambert, his body trembling.

Klatzky's name and address were printed on the front. There was no stamp. 'You received this today?'

'It was there when I got back.'

'Back from where?'

'I was out last night. Got in early this morning.' He looked at Lambert as if expecting a reprimand.

Lambert opened the envelope and pulled out a file of A4 papers. Each page had a colour photo of the same subject taken from a different angle. Lambert tapped the table with the knuckles of his left hand as he read through the file.

'It's him, Mike,' said Klatzky.

The subject was the deceased figure of an emaciated man. The skin of the corpse was a dull yellow. Wisps of frazzled hair clung to the man's cheek bones, matted together with a green-brown substance. The corpse's mouth was wide open, caught forever in a look of rictus surprise. Where the man's eyes should have been were two hollow sockets. Tendrils of skin and matter dripped down onto the man's face. Lambert recognised the Latin insignia carved intricately into the man's chest. He placed the file back in the envelope, wiping a bead of sweat from his brow.

'Well?' asked Klatzky.

'Where did you get this from?'

Klatzky poured more of the clear liquid into his cup. 'I told you. It was there this morning when I got back. Why the hell has this been sent to me, Mike?' he asked, loud enough to receive some disapproving looks from the young mothers.

Lambert rubbed his face. If he'd known what was in the envelope, then he would never have suggested meeting in such a public place. 'I'll talk to some people. See what I can find out. I'll need to keep this,' he said.

'But why was it sent to me, Mikey?'

'I don't know.' Lambert checked the address on the envelope. 'You're still in the same flat, over in East Ham?'

'Afraid so.'

'Have you seen anyone else recently?'

'You mean from Uni? No. You're the first one I've seen since the...' he hesitated. 'Since, the funeral.'

Lambert replayed the images in his head, trying to ignore the expectation etched onto Klatzky's face. The inscription on the victim's chest read:

*In oculis animus habitat.*

The lettering, smudged by leaking blood, had dried into thick maroon welts on the pale skin of the man's body. Lambert didn't need to see the man's eyeless sockets to work out the translation:

*The soul dwells in the eyes.*

They left the coffee house together. 'Do you have somewhere else you can go?' asked Lambert.

'Why? Do you think I'm next?' asked Klatzky.

Lambert wasn't sure what Klatzky had put in his coffee but the man was swaying from side to side. He placed his hand on the man's shoulder. 'Let's not panic. These might not have come from the murderer. But until we do find out where they came from, and why they were sent to you, it would be sensible to stay away from the flat.'

'Should we tell Billy's parents or something? Christ, what are they are going to think?'

Billy Nolan had been the ninth and, until now, last victim

of the so called Souljacker killer. A close friend of Lambert and Klatzky, Nolan was murdered in his final year at Bristol University where they had all studied. The killer had never been caught and everything Lambert had seen in the file suggested that he had started working again.

'Look, you need to get somewhere and rest up. Let me worry about the details.'

'I want to help, Mikey.'

'You can stay out of trouble. That will help the most. I'll contact you when I know something.' He grabbed Klatzky's hand and shook it. 'It'll be okay, Si.'

Klatzky's handshake was weak, his palm wet with sweat. He swayed for a second before stumbling across the road to a bar called The Blue Boar.

Lambert stood outside the coffee shop, his hand clutched tight to the envelope. Years ago Lambert would have jumped straight into the investigation. The responsible thing would be to locate the Senior Investigating Officer on the case, inform them that Klatzky had received the material. But he needed time to process the information, to decipher why Klatzky had received the photos.

He walked to Clockhouse station and caught a train to Charing Cross, his mind racing. Making sure no one could see him, he opened the envelope. He scanned each page in turn, studied every detail. The photographs were direct copies from a crime report. The photographer had captured the corpse from all angles. The camera zoomed in on the victim's wounds. The ragged skin around the eye sockets, the incision marks magnified in gruesome detail, the intricate detail of the Latin inscription, each letter meticulously carved into the victim's skin. It was definitely a professional job.

Reaching London, Lambert took the short walk to Covent Garden. His wife, Sophie, was waiting for him in a small bistro off the old market building. She sat near the entrance, head buried in a leather folio. 'Oh, hi,' she said, on seeing him.

'Hi, yourself.'

She shut the document she'd been reading. 'Shall we order?' she asked, business-like as usual.

They'd been married for twelve years. Sophie was half-French on her mother's side. A petite woman, she had short black hair, and a soft round face which made her look ten years younger than her actual age of thirty-nine.

They both ordered the fish of the day. 'So how was Simon?' she asked.

'Not great,' said Lambert.

'Well, don't keep me in suspense. What did he want?'

Absentmindedly, Lambert touched the document in his inside jacket pocket. 'Oh, nothing dramatic. He was thinking of putting together some sort of reunion.'

He could tell she knew he was lying. They ordered water to go with the fish and sat through the meal in companionable silence. Each avoiding discussing the reason they were there.

'Everything's booked,' she said, finally. 'The same church as last year. We can use the church hall afterwards. All the catering is organised.'

Lambert drank the water, cracking a fragment of ice which had dropped into his mouth. A shiver ran through his body as the cold water dripped down his throat. 'Okay,' he said, realising how useless the words sounded. How he was, even after all this time, still unable to deal with the enormity of the situation.

'We need to finalise the music,' said Sophie.

Lambert gripped his glass of water, tried to focus on something more positive. 'Do you remember that track she loved in the summer before she started school? She used to go crazy. Blondie, wasn't it? She used to pick up her tennis racket and play along. I can't remember for the life of me what it was called.'

Sophie beamed, reliving the memory. Then, in an instant, her eyes darkened. It had been two years since their daughter, Chloe, had died. They'd decided to hold a memorial service each year on Chloe's birthday. Sophie's mother had suggested they postpone it this year. She'd argued that rekindling the same memories every twelve months denied a necessary part of the grieving process. In principle Lambert agreed, but it was not a subject he could broach with Sophie. He blamed himself for Chloe's death, and though she insisted otherwise, he was sure Sophie did too.

Eventually they agreed on a small song list.

'I need to go,' said Sophie. She stood and kissed him on the cheek, a perfunctory habit devoid of emotion. At home, they slept in separate rooms rarely spending more than five minutes together. This was the first meal they'd shared in almost a year.

Lambert hadn't worked since Chloe's death. He'd been hospitalised, and received substantial compensation. The last time Sophie had raised the subject of him returning to work they'd argued. Now the matter was never discussed.

'I'll be home early this evening,' she said. 'Then I'm out for dinner.'

She loitered by the table and regarded him in the way only she could. Lambert saw love in the gesture, tinged with compassion and empathy. But what he saw most of all was pity.

After she left, he paid the bill and walked outside. He found a secluded spot and took out the manila envelope once more. The easiest thing would be to send the file to the authorities and forget Klatzky had ever given it to him. And if he hadn't just had lunch with Sophie, and seen that look of pity, that would have been his course.

Instead, he put the envelope back in his jacket and walked along the Strand. On a side street, he entered a small establishment he'd used in the past.

Inside, he purchased a pre-charged Pay As You Go mobile phone in cash.

From memory, he dialled a number he hadn't called in two years.

# CHAPTER TWO

As expected, the man didn't answer. Lambert left a message asking for a meeting. Ten minutes later he received a text message with an address and time.

Lambert caught the tube to Angel in Islington and located a set of rented offices. He showed his identification to the male receptionist but didn't mention the name of the man he was supposed to meet. The receptionist led him to a small office area. He entered a four-digit code on a side panel and ushered Lambert into the room. The room had the feel of a prison cell. It had no window, only four brick walls and a steel-framed door. Lambert sat on one of the three faux-leather office chairs situated around a rectangular glass table and studied the photos once more.

Glenn Tillman exploded into the room five minutes later. A bulldog of a man, almost as wide as he was tall, Tillman had a pouty, baby-like face which looked out of place on top of his heaving muscle-strewn body.

'I don't like to be summoned,' he said, as way of greeting.

'Good to see you too,' said Lambert. The last time he'd seen Tillman had been shortly after Chloe's funeral. Both men had agreed that Lambert should take some extended time away from work. Lambert hadn't heard from him since.

Lambert dropped the envelope onto the glass table. Tillman moved towards him and picked it up, his expression passive as he scanned the photos.

'And?' he said.

'I hoped I would have been informed if anything came in on this,' said Lambert.

Tillman sat, his breathing heavy. A blue striped tie bulged rhythmically against his thick neck. 'You don't work for us at the moment, Michael.'

'This relates directly to me, sir. It would have been a courtesy.'

Tillman studied the photos again. 'This goes back to your University days, doesn't it? I remember it from your file. What did the press call him, the Souljacker or something?' He put the file down. 'Look, this is the first I've heard of it. It must be with the local CID. It's not something that would come our way, you know that.'

'I want access,' said Lambert.

Tillman smirked. 'There's no access, Michael. If you're not working for us then no way.'

'Employ me then. Private contract.'

'We don't do that any more. We're part of the NCA now. Sort of,' he said, as an afterthought. The National Crime Agency had replaced SOCA, the Serious Organised Crime Agency, the previous year.

'Right,' said Lambert. Lambert had been working for SOCA when Tillman had recruited him. They'd previously worked together when Lambert had first joined CID. Tillman had been his first DI.

Tillman now headed a department known simply as The Group. It was a cross alliance with military intelligence. There had been five others in Lambert's team. Aside from Tillman, The Group comprised one DI and one DS from the MET, and two operatives from MI5. For the first time in his career, Lambert had signed the Official Secrets Act for work and received a security clearance level. Lambert had long suspected that there were a number of similar groups working independent from Tillman's collective.

'Look, sir. I don't want to push this but I need access.' He was taking a calculated risk speaking to his superior this way. It was not beyond Tillman to tell him where to go, to leave him in the room for twenty-four hours to dwell on his insolence.

Tillman lifted his hand to his face. 'You're calling it in?'

Tillman didn't really owe him anything, but his superior didn't see it that way. Lambert had protected him once and still held potentially incriminating evidence on the man. He would never betray Tillman, but Tillman was honour bound to repay the favour. 'I don't want it to be like that, but if it has to be that way.'

Tillman rubbed his left temple, A familiar gesture Lambert had seen countless times before. 'I will say you stole the access codes if it ever comes to light.'

'I realise that.'

'Then we're done, Michael. Unless you come back to us, it will be the last time you have access to The System.'

'Thank you, sir,' said Lambert, getting to his feet.

'I will email you the access codes within the next two

hours. Any work you do on this Souljacker business is yours alone. Make no records. Understand?'

'Sir.'

Tillman left the room without acknowledging him.

Lambert thanked the receptionist as he left the building. He doubted the man had any idea who he was, or who Tillman was for that matter. Lambert savoured the fresh air once outside, buoyed by the meeting. He'd thought he'd have to argue his case for access to The System but Tillman had given in almost immediately. He'd even given a suggestion of Lambert returning to work for him in the future.

The access codes arrived two hours later. Lambert was back at his desk in his home office, a three-storey Edwardian house in Beckenham, Kent, which bordered south-east London. Before him, information scrolled across six computer monitors. It had been a long time since he'd last activated them.

The System had been the reason Lambert had signed the OSA. As far as he was aware, only a handful of people outside The Group knew of its existence. The System was an amalgamation of existing computer systems and databases, as well as something else entirely. The System had direct access to a number of worldwide criminal databases including HOLMES and the PNC in the UK, and limited access to databases used by Interpol and European forces. In addition, The System could access the backend of nearly all social media sites.

Lambert experienced a rush of adrenalin as he logged into The System with codes sent to him by Tillman. He spent a few minutes acclimatising to the new layout, and exhaled sharply as he accessed details of the new Souljacker murder.

The case appeared on HOLMES, the system used by the police to record details on major crimes.

A neighbour had discovered the body of Terrence Vernon five days ago, in a two-bedroom top floor flat in an area called Southville, a mile from the city centre of Bristol. The smell of the corpse had alerted the neighbour who had duly informed the police. The Senior Investigating Officer was Detective Superintendent Rush, though it was apparent that the chief investigator was Detective Inspector Sarah May.

The pathologist's initial report suggested that the deceased had endured every part of the attack, including the removal of his eyes, the man's eventual death resulting from a cut to his carotid artery. It had been no real leap to link the killing to the notorious Souljacker murders, the last of which had taken place eighteen years ago.

Lambert opened the window in the office. He could still picture Billy Nolan. In their last year at University together, his small group of friends had all managed to secure a place at the halls of residence. Nolan had lived six doors down from Lambert on the fifth floor.

It was Lambert who had broken down Nolan's door that night. Nolan sprawled on his bed, giant bloody holes where his eyes should have been. Lambert had recognised it was Latin carved into his friend's body but couldn't translate it. He'd stared, dumbfounded, at the lifeless form, hoping it was some twisted joke being played on him. Then the smell had overwhelmed him and he'd struggled into the corridor and vomited.

Lambert shuddered. Similar scenes played on the computer screens now. Photos of Terrence Vernon's corpse scrolled across each screen, lying askew on his bedroom floor, the two gaping holes in his skull looking too wide to have ever held human eyes. Next, the close-up pictures of the Latin, *In oculis animus habitat.* Like on all the previous victims, each letter was carved into Vernon's chest in faultless detail, suggesting the killer had spent hours on the inscription.

Lambert recalled the fallout from Billy's Nolan's death, the number of lives forever affected by the senseless murder. He remembered the desolate look on the faces of Nolan's parents as they arrived at the University. The students who had witnessed the sight of Billy's disfigured corpse, who would never be quite the same again, who would always equate University with that one defining moment. He counted himself amongst their number.

Sophie knocked on the office door and Lambert closed the screens with a single punch of the keypad.

'Hungry?'

'I had something earlier, thanks.'

'Working?' asked Sophie, unable to hide the hope in her voice.

'Sort of.'

She hesitated by the door. 'That's good.' She was holding back, wanted to find out more but was probably afraid of how he might respond.

Lambert stared ahead at the blank computer screens, desperate to get on with work, ashamed that he didn't know how to talk to his estranged wife any longer.

'Okay, just popping out for dinner.'

'See you in the morning,' said Lambert.

Sophie shut the office door and Lambert returned to the computer screens. He had to blank out what was happening in his marriage for the time being. He returned to the screens and read through the case details uploaded onto the HOLMES system.

*In oculis animus habitat. The soul dwells in the eyes.*

During the weeks following Nolan's murder there had been much discussion as to the meaning of those words. The SIO at the time, DCI Julian Hastings, had questioned Lambert about his understanding of the words. Lambert had studied Latin in school but couldn't translate the words exactly without looking it up.

Billy Nolan had been the ninth and, supposedly, final Souljacker victim. Now, from nowhere, the killer was back.

From her notes, Lambert read that DI May had begun researching the older cases. The first victim, Clive Hale, had been murdered over twenty two years ago, the next eight victims falling foul of the Souljacker over a period of four years. May had assigned a number of junior officers the duty of trawling through witness reports and suspect interviews. During the Nolan investigation, a local surgeon, Peter Randall, had been the chief suspect, but the case had never gone anywhere near the courts. There had been no forensic evidence and Randall had a clear alibi for the time of the murder. It had been the only significant arrest there had ever been on the case.

Lambert had kept in contact with DCI Hastings after the murder. Hastings had offered him advice on joining the force. Now a retired Chief Superintendent, Hastings had stayed obsessed with the Souljacker cases even into retirement. If May had any sense, Hastings would be the first person she contacted.

Lambert clicked a button on his keyboard and sat back in his office chair. DI Sarah May's file on the latest killing played through his six computer screens in a reel of information.

Lambert sat transfixed and absorbed the material. He often worked this way, viewing the details from an abstract position searching for a key word, sentence, or picture that would change everything.

The same age as Lambert, Vernon had worked as a retail manager for a large supermarket in the Cribbs Causeway area of Bristol. Described by family, friends, and colleagues as a shy, awkward sort of person, his hard work ethic had helped him reach a reasonable level in his career. Vernon was single. He had divorced parents and no siblings. He had strong links with a local evangelical church, Gracelife Bristol, the minister of which, Neil Landsdale, had described Vernon as a hard-working and selfless member of his congregation who 'would be sorely missed'.

Lambert watched unblinking as the pages scrolled across the screens. He read and reread the information until something made him pause. It was a picture of Vernon, taken with his work colleagues at the supermarket. Vernon towered over everyone else. Thin and ungainly in an ill-fitting shiny polyester suit, he was clean shaven with short cropped hair, a well-defined face with high cheekbones, and strong jaw.

Lambert couldn't make out the colour of his eyes. He stared hard at the image of Vernon, a memory returning to him. He clicked onto another screen and accessed details on Vernon's personal file. He scanned down the file and stopped at Terrence's mother, Sandra Vernon. He clicked on her name.

It took him less than sixty seconds to find out what he was looking for.

Sandra Vernon's married name was Sandra Haydon. She had officially divorced Terrence's father, Roger Haydon fifteen years ago, though they had separated when Terrence was a child.

Lambert reloaded the photo of the victim, Terrence Vernon. Lambert cursed under his breath. Terrence must have changed his surname to his mother's maiden name.

At University, Lambert had known him as Terrence Haydon.

# CHAPTER THREE

Lambert emailed DI May requesting a meeting for the following day. He didn't share any information on the photos he'd received from Klatzky. He wanted to meet the woman face to face. After which he would decide if he wanted to take his personal investigation any further.

The fact that Klatzky had been sent the photos was obviously hugely significant but Lambert needed to know why he'd been sent them before he shared the details with anyone. His first thought was that the photos were a warning but the more he thought about it the less likely that seemed.

It came down to the sender. Lambert's gut told him the killer had sent the photos and there was no logical reason for him to send a warning. It was possible the killer was playing a game with Klatzky. Like Lambert, Klatzky had been there the day Billy Nolan's body had been found. Klatzky had been closer to Billy than anyone, and his life had spiralled out of control ever since Nolan's death. Why the killer wanted to involve Klatzky now after all these years was anyone's guess at the moment but at least it was a starting point for Lambert to pin his investigation on. A second starting point was the possibility that the killer was using Klatzky to lure Lambert into action. A more worrying thought had also occurred to him: that somehow the killer was attempting to set them up.

A nervous energy ran through him as he printed up relevant parts of the file. It was good to be back working, even on something so close to him. He took the files to the small bedroom at the top of the house. It was sparsely decorated with a single bed, desk, and chair, the flat screen television which hung on the wall taking up most of the space in the room. He flicked through the channels, unable to find anything of interest. He checked his email on his phone noticing that Klatzky had emailed him five times since their meeting, becoming more incoherent with each email. By the final email his words made little sense.

Lambert switched off the television and closed his eyes. His body hummed with tension, his chest tight as if an invisible weight pushed down on him. Eventually, the first flicker occurred. A fiery orange glow appeared to his left and blossomed into a collage of bright colour taking over his entire visual field. Infinite shades of red, yellow, and orange began to fade as his breathing slowed and he fell asleep.

He slept for three hours and reached Paddington station by six a.m. The station already teemed with commuters. Lambert booked his ticket and ordered a large black coffee from one of the shops in the large open-spaced concourse. He stretched his legs, alert and awake despite the meagre hours of sleep.

Lambert had survived most of his adult life on three to four hours a night and hadn't suffered any detrimental side effects until four years ago when the hallucinations started.

They occurred when he was overly tired or stressed. He had self-diagnosed his condition as a rare form of narcolepsy. It was something he'd never had checked out, fearing that an official diagnosis would affect his work. He had learned that the hallucinations were a signal that he was ready for sleep. He could control them now, to an extent. Unfortunately, that had not always been the case.

Lambert drank the bitter coffee, impatient for the train to arrive. May had yet to respond to his request for a meeting. He would give her until nine a.m. to reply to his email or his first destination would be her police station. Lambert watched the commuters and wondered if his own face mirrored the dull and sullen faces which hurried by him, everyone impatient and tired.

A different type of figure emerged from the set of escalators which rose from the underground. The unsteady figure of a man dressed in faded jeans and tattered leather jacket staggered towards him.

'Great,' whispered Lambert to himself. He considered hiding from the figure but Klatzky had already spotted him.

'Mikey,' he said, a little too loud. 'I knew you would be here.' Klatzky embraced him.

Competing odours overwhelmed Lambert. Sweat, cheap aftershave and stale nicotine were all linked by the reek of alcohol. Lambert kept his hands by his sides, tried to breathe through his mouth. 'What the hell are you doing here, Simon?' Despite the revulsion at Klatzky's state, Lambert could not help but admire the man for finding him.

'I knew Bristol would be the logical place for you to start,' said Klatzky, slurring half of his words. 'You never sleep, so it would have to be the first train. I'm coming with you.'

Lambert took a couple of steps back. 'You're not going

anywhere, except home. Do you have any idea what you look like? What you smell like for that matter? I wouldn't even sit in the same carriage as you let alone share a train journey.'

'I need to come with you, Mikey. Look, I'm not afraid to admit it but I'm scared. He's back. I want to know what's happening, why he sent me the pictures. You told me not to go home, so I didn't.' Klatzky eyes darted around the station, as if he was surprised by his location.

Lambert shook his head. 'You've been out all night?'

Klatzky shrugged his shoulders, a grin spreading across his face.

This was the last thing he needed. 'Jesus. Listen, I'll keep you informed. Where are you staying? Go and sleep it off. It'll do you no good coming with me to Bristol.'

'I need to know, Mikey,' insisted Klatzky. He placed a shaking hand on Lambert's shoulder, the leathery skin laced with wrinkles and a fine layer of black hair, the hand of a much older man. Lambert tried not to recoil from the touch.

The train was about to depart. Lambert took another step back and Klatzky's shaking hand fell away. If the killer had sent Klatzky the file to get Lambert involved then the fear he saw in his friend's eyes was at least partly his responsibility. 'Okay, Simon. You can come with me but you can't interfere. Is that understood?'

'You're a saint, Mikey,' said Klatzky.

'Shall we go then?'

'I need a ticket,' said Klatzky.

'Oh I see. I'll get you one on the train.'

Mercifully, Klatzky fell asleep before the train pulled out of Paddington station. He collapsed in a heap, his frail body lying at an awkward angle in the seats opposite Lambert.

Lambert opened his holdall and searched its contents. He pulled out a newspaper, and the file he had compiled on the Souljacker murders. There was still nothing from May on his phone. The conductor approached and Lambert purchased a return ticket for Klatzky with his credit card.

Klatzky snored himself awake as the train pulled into Swindon. His body spasmed, his head cracking against the underside of the table with a thud. Lambert tried not to laugh as the man composed himself.

'How long have I been asleep?' said Klatzky, rubbing his head.

'Fifty minutes or so.'

Klatzky dusted himself down, his aged leather jacket creaking at each movement. He shuffled himself into position, sitting opposite Lambert. A waft of pungent air drifted across the table.

'Your ticket,' said Lambert.

'Thanks, I'll pay you back.'

Lambert stopped the woman pushing a drinks trolley down the aisle of the carriage.

'Coffee,' groaned Klatzky.

'Make that two,' said Lambert. They sat for a while in silence. Klatzky wincing as he took the occasional sip of coffee.

'What happened to us eh, Mikey?' said Klatzky a few minutes later.

Lambert was reading one of the three books he'd brought with him, a mostly useless textbook on lucid sleeping. 'What do you mean?'

'Don't you remember those train journeys we used to take to Bristol on our way to University? We'd be half cut by now.'

'You are half cut.'

'Maybe,' said Klatzky. 'What happened to you, anyway? You were so happy go lucky then. You didn't take anything seriously, not even your degree. Now look at you.'

'That was twenty years ago, Simon.' Lambert linked his hands together and rested his chin on them, staring at Klatzky.

In response, Klatzky leant towards him. Pointing his finger, he said, 'We all grow up, Michael, but you changed. You've changed intrinsically as a person.'

Lambert laughed, but felt his facial muscles tighten as his face reddened. 'Intrinsically? What are you talking about, Simon?

Klatzky slumped back in his seat. 'If you don't know what I'm talking about then there's no point in explaining,' he said. He drank the last of his coffee, screwing his eyes shut as he downed the dregs.

Lambert thought about continuing the bizarre argument, realising it was pointless arguing with Klatzky when he was in this mood. He opened his newspaper and spent the rest of the journey skimming through the despairing stories, his thoughts constantly returning to the file in his jacket pocket and what it all meant. At face value, it didn't make much sense. Serial killers like the Souljacker didn't just take eighteen years off between killings. If it was the same killer then there must have been a reason for the killer to have stopped in the first place, and more importantly a catalyst which had propelled him back to work.

Once in Bristol, they ordered breakfast at a small greasy spoon café outside Temple Meads station. Klatzky's head drooped as they waited for their orders, his hangover clearly reaching its peak.

A teenage girl in a pink apron placed their breakfasts on the table. She grinned, the white of her teeth obscured by a thick metal brace. Piling his fork with a mixture of sausage, bacon and egg, Klatzky perked up. With his mouth half full he mumbled, 'So what are our plans for today?'

'Well, I plan to go to the University and have a look at our old halls of residence. And if I haven't heard back from her I'm going to call the lead investigator on the case.'

'Are we going to get a hotel?' asked Klatzky, slicing through an egg yolk smothered in ketchup.

'No, I want to be out of this place by the end of the day.'

'Oh come on, Mikey, we could visit some old haunts. For old times' sake.'

Lambert turned his face to the side, stretching his neck muscles. 'It's not a jolly, Simon. You asked me to help. This is work for me.' He already regretted allowing Klatzky to accompany him on the journey, and sensed things were only going to get worse.

Klatzky returned to his breakfast, sulking like a scolded child. 'I was thinking of calling the others,' he said, a couple of minutes later. He finished his breakfast, wiping his plate clean with a thin slice of white bread. He looked Lambert in the eyes for the first time since they'd left the train.

'That's not a good idea,' said Lambert.

'Why not? We haven't all been together for years,' said Klatzky.

There had been six of them in their group. They'd spent their three years at University together as the tightest of cliques, all deciding to reapply for halls in the third year. 'There's a reason for that, Simon.' Lambert placed some money on the table and left the café before Klatzky could argue further.

Over the years, Klatzky had been the only one who had tried to keep the group together. There had been the occasional impromptu reunion every few months after they'd graduated but the get-togethers had never been successful. They would initially start off well but after a few drinks it always became apparent that everyone was avoiding talking about Billy Nolan; it would reach the point where someone would mention his name just to break the tension.

Then the bad memories would return and the drinking would intensify until everyone reached a state of maudlin drunkenness which would occasionally descend into bouts of violence.

The others had all managed to put the Nolan incident behind them to one extent or another. Lambert knew getting the group together again would only reignite bad memories.

They caught a taxi from the long line of black cabs outside the station. 'You're a bit young to be students,' said the rotund taxi driver, after being told their destination.

'We're alumni,' said Lambert, his tone suggesting that all forms of communication between the driver and his two passengers should now cease. Lambert had only returned to Bristol occasionally over the last eighteen years, mainly for work. The city had transformed in that time but the changes had been gradual. Lambert couldn't date any of the buildings. It was only when the taxi pulled up outside their destination that he felt a stab of nostalgia. Klatzky was almost tearful as they left the car.

'Can't you feel it in your bones, Mikey?' he said, stretching his arms out as if he wanted to embrace the building.

Memories came to Lambert. Glimpsed images of the numerous nights out he'd enjoyed with his friends, of the girls he'd kissed, each memory tainted with the image of Billy Nolan, dead in his room.

Inside, Lambert had to produce his old warrant card before the grey-haired man behind the security desk would allow them entry into their old hall of residence. They took the unsteady lift to the fifth floor, Lambert enduring the odour which resulted from Klatzky's lack of personal hygiene. 'When did you last shower?'

'I was out all night before I met you at Paddington.'

'Of course you were,' said Lambert. Lambert had yet to tell Klatzky about Terrence Haydon. Klatzky was in too fragile a state at the moment to take in the news that he'd once known the latest victim.

None of them had known Haydon well. He'd been an odd character who, like the report suggested, kept himself to himself. The other students had considered Haydon as somewhat of an eccentric. He'd studied Religious Studies and always carried a Bible with him, though Lambert could never recall him trying to push his views on anyone. He wasn't even sure Haydon had been that religious. He couldn't remember him being a member of the Christian Union.

Although the halls had been refurbished they looked essentially the same to Lambert. More memories came to him, mostly childish recollections of late-night drinking, water fights in the corridor, desperate early mornings of coffee-fuelled revision and the occasional romantic encounter. Klatzky was once again close to tears. Lambert knew the man's hangover was intensifying his emotional response but it didn't make it any easier to endure.

'Why are we here, Mikey?'

'I thought it would do good to reacquaint myself,' said Lambert. He didn't want to explain to Klatzky that he wanted to revisit the beginning from a professional viewpoint. He had been in his early twenties when Nolan's life had been taken. Lambert had been just another dazed student at the time. Although it was nearly twenty years later, Lambert thought there might be the opportunity to see something afresh. Something he may have missed, or had not been looking for all those years before.

A middle-aged woman in a blue checked apron stopped them both. 'Can I help you?' she asked, in a deep West Country accent.

Lambert flashed his old warrant card. 'I wanted to see Room 516,' he said. When the cleaner showed him to a room halfway down the corridor Lambert realised the room numbers had been rearranged. The fifth floor had a rectangular corridor and Nolan's room had been on the left-hand side corner with the window facing east onto the main road. Lambert followed his memory to where Nolan's room should have been. On the door where Nolan had once lived hung a sign marked *Storage Cupboard*.

'How long has this room been a cupboard?' asked Lambert.

'It's always been a cupboard,' said the woman.

'Don't be ridiculous,' said Klatzky indignantly.

'Listen, I've only been working here six years, love,' said the woman.

'It's fine, it's fine,' said Lambert. 'Could we possibly look inside?'

'Suit yourself,' said the woman, producing a key. 'I haven't all day, mind you.'

Shelves full of cleaning material and crisp folded sheets filled out the room. It bore no resemblance to the untidy and poster-ridden room which had once been Billy Nolan's. The change of use had destroyed the room's potency. Lambert had feared he would be overcome with more memories of that day. Now it was hard to believe the incident had ever occurred in such a space.

'Let's go,' said Klatzky. 'This place is giving me the creeps.' His eyes sagged towards his cheeks, his lips trembling beneath the random spikes of black and grey hair which sprung from his sallow face.

'Simon, go and get a coffee or something down in the cafeteria. I'm going to have a look around. I'll meet you in ten minutes.'

Klatzky slumped off towards the lift. Lambert thanked the cleaner who locked the store cupboard giving him a confused and pitiful look. Once Klatzky was inside the lift, Lambert walked up the stairs to the sixth floor. He made a full circuit of the floor but couldn't summon the memory of where Haydon had resided. A nagging sense told him that Haydon had lived almost directly above Billy Nolan but he couldn't be sure. It felt too much of a coincidence. Before joining Klatzky for coffee, Lambert called Bristol CID and asked to be put through to DI May.

'Can I ask what it's regarding?' enquired a female voice on the other end of the line.

'Tell her it's about the Terrence Vernon case,' said Lambert. Thirty seconds later a strong deep female voice said, 'DI May, how can I help?'

Lambert explained his position, telling May he was a former police officer who had important information about the Vernon case. Lambert presumed May had already discovered that Terrence Vernon was originally called Terrence Haydon, but wasn't about to discuss the matter over the phone.

'Where are you now?' asked May.

'In Clifton.'

'Okay, there's a little café on The Triangle called Liberties. Could you meet me there at midday?'

'Done,' said Lambert.

# CHAPTER FOUR

Klatzky sat alone in the student cafeteria, woefully out of place. Facedown, he nursed a small coffee occasionally giving the students a suspicious look. He was at once vulnerable and unsettling, and the café's patrons subconsciously sat as far away from him as possible.

After Klatzky declined his offer of a second coffee, Lambert ordered a large black Americano from a young man behind the counter. Klatzky looked up at him with sullen eyes when he returned. 'I thought I'd enjoy being here, Mikey, but there are way too many memories. Being here makes it feel like it happened yesterday. I can remember everything, what that sicko did to his body.' Klatzky sipped at his coffee. 'Christ, and the smell, Mikey. I can taste it now more than ever. Do you ever feel like that? It's part of me now. The blood and the smell...what was that stuff called?'

'The incense?'

'Yeah.' He took another longer sip of his coffee as if trying to drown out the memory. 'One good thing came out of it though,' he quipped, 'I never went back to church again. Too

much incense in Catholic churches. I don't even feel the need
to go to confession.'

'Small mercies, I guess,' said Lambert. Pontifical incense
had been found on the body of each Souljacker victim, and
Billy Nolan had been no exception. Traces of the incense,
which contained frankincense, matched that used by a
number of Catholic churches in the country. However, the
substance was freely available so it had proved impossible for
any trace to be made.

'Listen, Si, I have a meeting later with the officer in charge
of the case. I have some information that she may or may not
know.'

'Okay,' said Klatzky.

'The body they found last week, the body in the pictures
you showed me, were of somebody called Terrence Vernon.'
Lambert tensed waiting for Klatzky's response.

'Terrence?'

'Yes, Terrence. I found out last night that Terrence Vernon
was using his mother's maiden name as a surname. He used
to be called Terrence Haydon. Do you remember Terrence
Haydon, Si?'

'Mad Terry?' Klatzky's face fell, his eyes wide in recogni-
tion. 'He killed Mad Terry? Fucking hell, Mikey. What does
this mean? What the hell's going on?' His words came out in
short, rapid bursts, oblivious to the other people in the
room.

'Keep it down, Si,' said Lambert, through gritted teeth. A
few of the students looked in their direction. Mad Terry had
been the uninspired nickname given to Terrence Haydon
whilst at University. The nickname resulted from a few eccentric behaviours, such as walking with long, exaggerated steps
as he made his way around. 'I don't know. It's partly why I

need to see DI May. There are so many possibilities at this juncture it's not worth hypothesising.'

Klatzky gripped Lambert's wrists, his hands sweaty. 'But Billy hardly knew Mad Terry, what's this to do with anything?'

Lambert unpeeled Klatzky's fingers, and, grimacing, wiped the sweat off onto the plastic table covering. 'It could mean anything or nothing,' he said, softening his voice. 'Maybe the killer thought Haydon knew something about him.'

'After all this time?'

'It's a possibility. Perhaps Haydon contacted the authorities. There's no way for me to know until I look into it in more detail.'

'What if the killer's coming after everyone involved in Billy's killing? Everyone who knew him?'

'Don't be dramatic, you need to snap out of this. If he's going to kill someone once every eighteen years there's a good chance that we're all going to be safe. Listen, I need to go. I'm not sure how long I'll be but I'll call you when I'm finished. Try to get some rest somewhere.'

'Where do you suggest?' asked Klatzky.

'I don't know. Find a sofa. But stay away from the bars.'

'Any other orders?'

'No.'

Lambert reached the coffee shop thirty minutes early. Like London, Bristol basked in the heat of the Indian summer. A number of people sat outside the glass-fronted café. One of the crowd, a woman with shoulder-length black hair, stood up as Lambert walked towards the entrance. 'Mr Lambert?' she said.

Lambert turned to face the woman. 'Yes?'

'I'm DI May. Sarah.'

'How did you know who I was?'

'Forgive me,' said May, not once taking her gaze away from him. 'Can I get you a coffee and perhaps we can go inside and talk.'

'Decaf, thanks,' said Lambert.

A blast of cold air hit Lambert as he entered the high-ceilinged coffee shop, at first refreshing then uncomfortable. DI May directed him to a small booth with high wooden benches. She returned with two drinks and smiled as she sat down opposite him. Her large brown eyes shone bright, full of confidence and intelligence. She wasn't wearing make-up and Lambert wondered if her looks were a benefit or hindrance in her professional life. From his experience, he imagined it was probably a bit of both.

'So tell me DI May...'

'Sarah, please,' said the woman with a soft, yet firm voice.

'Sarah. Tell me what you found out about me?'

DI May leant forward in her chair, her gaze remained steady, never once leaving Lambert's eyes. Most people would have found her glare unnerving, would have felt obliged to look away, but Lambert matched her look. She spoke with a sly amusement. 'Well, first of all, possibly most importantly, I know you're a friend of the last Souljacker victim, Billy Nolan. In fact, Mr Lambert ...'

'Please, Michael.'

May squinted her eyes. 'Michael. You were initially a suspect.'

Lambert crossed his arms, deciding not to answer.

'Of course, you were one of many potential suspects and were cleared very early on in the case.'

Lambert's eyes widened, prompting the DI to continue.

'After graduation you were accepted into the accelerated programme, where you excelled.' She nodded in admiration, and let out a small laugh. 'You moved up the ranks and reached DCI.'

Impressed by her research, Lambert didn't interrupt.

'And then the mystery.'

'The mystery?'

'Yes, six years ago your work becomes classified. I received a phone call from a Chief Super this morning for trying to access the details.'

'Which one?'

'Tillman.'

'Right.'

'So can you fill in those blanks for me, Michael?'

'Afraid not. As the file says, classified.' Lambert hadn't given much thought to his personnel file before though it was obvious that his work with Tillman was classified. The blanks coincided from when he'd joined The Group. He made a mental note to access it later on The System. Although government sanctioned, in many ways the organisation was a law unto themselves. Their remit had been to investigate politically sensitive cases, and as such the need to avoid public scrutiny. It had been a tough transition for Lambert moving from normal CID to The Group. He'd found out early on that it was a balancing act. They'd worked out of the same offices as other task forces, and were supposedly subject to the same governing rules, but at times Lambert had been given leeway he'd never experienced before. The small team had been issued firearms and had received military intelligence-level training. Lambert had known it was somewhat of an experiment, and from his meeting yesterday Tillman wasn't about to tell him if things had changed.

'But apart from that, you've done very well, Sarah.'

She shot him a glance, but he could tell she knew he was teasing her. 'So what can you tell me, Michael?'

Lambert didn't want to be too pushy at the outset. 'I've been doing a little reading on the case,' he said.

'Naturally,' said May.

'I was particularly interested in the victim, Terrence Vernon.' He studied May for a response. If she was surprised she didn't show it.

'What about him?'

'I was wondering how much you knew about him.'

'How much information do you have on the case?'

'As I said, I've read some notes.'

'I understood you are not active at the moment. I read something on your file about an absence of leave?' said May. The words were matter of fact, contained no hostility.

'Something like that. I take it you've made the same connection I'd had about Mr Vernon.'

'You're talking about Mr Vernon's other name?'

'Yes.'

'It was his mother who let it slip. I spent some time with her. She told me about her divorce and how Terrence had changed his name back from Haydon to Vernon after leaving University. From there, we made the link with Billy Nolan. They were at University together. He lived one floor above Billy Nolan.' She paused. 'One floor above you.'

Lambert paused, assessing the underlying words. 'I needn't have bothered you, then,' he said.

'You're not bothering me. So tell me what else you know.'

'Not much more than that,' replied Lambert.

May's face contorted into a half smile, half frown. 'Oh come on, we're not going to play those games are we?'

Lambert shrugged. 'From what I can see it's highly probably that it's the same killer,' he said, checking no one was eavesdropping.

'Of course, you saw the original body. Your friend Nolan.'

Lambert thought back to the day when they'd kicked down Billy Nolan's door. Nolan's corpse with its bloodied sockets, lying naked on the bed. The smell, a terrifying mixture of death and decay, not fully masked by the overpowering perfume of the incense. Klatzky had been right. That smell was part of Lambert too. He could taste it now at the back of his throat. He took a large swig of his coffee mirroring Klatzky's earlier actions. Once he'd composed himself he said, 'The carving is the same. Identical. And the eyes. He was alive when they were removed?' he asked, knowing the answer.

May pursed her lips. 'They haven't been recovered. Like the others. Were Nolan and Haydon friends at University?'

'No. We all knew Terrence but he wasn't what we'd call a friend.'

And what was he like as a person?' May raised her eyebrows and tilted her head. A practised gesture which had no doubt obtained many a confession from helpless suspects.

'I'm sure you know all this but he was bit of a strange one.'

'Mad Terry,' said May, surprising him once more.

'Mad Terry. He was a nice enough guy, though. Intelligent. I assume he was hardworking because he was always at lectures. Never slept in. Hardly went out.'

'Any enemies?'

'No. People talked about him behind his back obviously,

me included I'm afraid. He wasn't a threat to anyone and no one had any grievance with him.'

'No altercations with Nolan?'

'Not as far as I'm aware. I would say it is highly unlikely.'

May ordered another coffee from the counter. Lambert asked for a glass of water, his bloodstream thick with caffeine. When she returned he tried to take the initiative. 'So what are you working on at the moment?' he asked.

'Normal procedures. We're looking into Haydon's church. As before, there was incense at the crime scene so we've contacted local churches to see if any amounts have gone missing. But the problem with these guys is that they just don't have strong stock control.' She raised her eyebrows again, a completely different look to before. The gesture softened her face and made Lambert feel like she was being companionable.

'We're crosschecking the other murders too but the connection between this murder and Billy Nolan's is our main focus at present. In fact if you hadn't found me there was a good chance that I'd have had to find you.'

'How can I help now?' asked Lambert.

'Maybe you could stick around for a bit. I could do with some insight on the Nolan murders, if that wouldn't affect you too much? Obviously I would prefer it if you didn't conduct your own investigation.' Her eyes narrowed, Lambert understanding the warning. She hesitated for a beat, the first sign of indecisiveness he'd seen. 'Perhaps we could meet for dinner this evening?' she said.

'Sure,' said Lambert, a little quicker than he would have liked.

DI May stood up to leave. 'It was a pleasure meeting you,' she said, shaking his hand.

'I'll see you this evening,' said Lambert. He relaxed as he watched May cross the floor of the coffee shop. The encounter had surprised him. May was more open than he'd expected, and he imagined how easy it would be to work with her.

As he was about to look away, May stopped and turned. 'Oh, Michael. Please feel free to bring along Mr Klatzky this evening as well if you wish.'

**DEAD EYED**
DCI Lambert book 1

Gritty, complex and effortlessly chilling, Brolly's *Dead Eyed* is a grisly crime thriller that will keep you on the edge of your seat.

**DCI Michael Lambert thought he'd closed his last case...**

Yet when he's passed a file detailing a particularly gruesome murder, Michael knows that this is no ordinary killer at work.

The removal of the victim's eyes and the Latin inscription carved into the chest is the chilling calling-card of the 'soul jacker': a cold-blooded murderer who struck close to Michael once before, twenty-five years ago.

Now the long-buried case is being re-opened, and Michael is determined to use his inside knowledge to finally bring the killer to justice. But as the body count rises, Michael realises that his own links to the victims could mean that he is next on the killer's list...

**The gripping first novel in a thrilling new crime series by Matt Brolly. Perfect for fans of Tony Parsons, Lee Child and Angela Marsons.**

# DEAD LUCKY
## DCI Lambert book 2

A fast-paced crime-thriller, full of chilling twists, turns and grisly surprises, Matt Brolly's *Dead Lucky* will have you gripped from beginning to end!

**DCI Michael Lambert is back...**

When a woman is murdered, the twisted killer forcing her husband to watch her slow and painful death, DCI Michael Lambert knows that his next case might be his toughest yet. And when a second set of killings are discovered, with exactly the same MO, the race is on the find the lethal sociopath before he strikes again.

But Lambert never expected to receive an anonymous call from the killer. This time, it's personal: if Lambert doesn't find the murderer soon, his own loved ones will be next...

**DEAD EMBERS**
DCI Lambert book 3

**An explosive fire. A double murder. And that's just the start**

When **DCI Michael Lambert** is called out to an apparent house fire, he knows it can't be routine. Instead he finds the remains of a burnt house, a traumatised child and two corpses - one of whom is a senior police officer.

Lambert's got other problems. Anti-corruption are onto his boss. His relationships is on the rocks. He can't get over his ex-wife and he keeps blacking out.

But when a detective has been murdered the stakes are too high to get distracted. All is not as it seems. As the investigation continues Lambert realises he is getting drawn into something altogether bigger and more terrifying than he could ever have imagined...

**Trust no one...**

## DEAD TIME
DCI Lambert book 4

Someone is recreating murders from the past; from DCI Lambert's past
A man is found electrocuted in his bath. Accident? Suicide? Apparently not. Attached to the body is a handwritten note; all it says is '**DCI Lambert**'. And something about the case rings a bell...
Lambert, shaken by past and present, is put on notice when a major prisoner escapes. Is there a connection? And why are MI5 getting involved? Before the investigation is over, Lambert will be pushed to his very limits... And beyond.
How far would you go for justice? And what would you do to save your family?

**The extraordinary new crime thriller from bestseller Matt Brolly is perfect for fans of Robert Bryndza, Joy Ellis and Angela Marsons.**